Julius Lloyd

The Life of Sir Philip Sidney

Julius Lloyd

The Life of Sir Philip Sidney

ISBN/EAN: 9783337094706

Printed in Europe, USA, Canada, Australia, Japan

Cover: Foto ©Raphael Reischuk / pixelio.de

More available books at **www.hansebooks.com**

THE
LIFE OF
SIR PHILIP SIDNEY.

BY

JULIUS LLOYD. M.A.

"His life was gentle; and the elements
So mixed in him, that Nature might ſtand up,
And ſay to all the world, ' This was a man.' "

LONDON:

LONGMAN, GREEN, LONGMAN, ROBERTS,

AND GREEN.

1862.

The Right of Tranſlation is reſerved.

PREFACE.

HORT Memoirs of Sir Philip Sidney are numerous; but his admirable character, no lefs than his great fame, demands a fuller account of his life. This was undertaken by Southey in 1804, as appears from his Diary. Unhappily, Southey never completed his biography. In 1808, Dr. Zouch publifhed, in a quarto volume, a mafs of interefting particulars about Sidney. As a memoir, however, Zouch's book is by no means fatisfactory; and fince it was written, much light has been thrown on the times of Elizabeth. The letters edited by Wright, Ellis, Murdin, Bruce, Gray, and Pears have been of effential fervice in the compofition of the prefent work. Mr. Motley's Hiftory of the Netherlands is not only valuable for its learned and picturefque expofition of European politics, but alfo contains fome curious notices of Sidney from unpublifhed fources. In addition to thefe, I have found feveral new facts by confulting the MSS. preferved at the State Paper Office, with the courteous affiftance which is given to ftudents there.

Where it has appeared to be requifite, I have cited authorities. But the following books have been fo conftantly in my hands, that it would be fuperfluous to have referred to them in ordinary cafes :—The Life of the renowned Sir Philip Sidney, by Sir Fulke Greville, Lord Brooke (edition of 1652). The Sidney Papers, edited, with Memoirs, by Arthur Collins, 2 vols. 1746. Sir P. Sidney's Mifcellaneous Works, edited, with a Life, by Wm. Gray. Oxford, 1829. Sidney's Correfpondence with Languet, tranflated and edited by Steuart A. Pears, D.D. Lond. 1845. Dr. Pears has added an excellent biographical preface.

Several portraits of Sidney are in the poffeffion of Lord De L'Ifle at Penfhurft. Among the pictures at Warwick Caftle is a beautiful head of Sidney, which was the property of the firft Lord Brooke. The Woburn picture is well known from the engraving in Lodge and Harding's collection. Other portraits are enumerated by correfpondents of "Notes and Queries," March 12, 1859, and Oct. 20, 1860. The engraving prefixed to Zouch's Memoirs is altogether a blunder. It is probably neither a likenefs of Sidney, nor a picture by Velafquez, who was born after Sidney's death.

During the progrefs of this volume through the prefs, its publication has been anticipated by that of a copious Memoir of Sir Philip Sidney by Mr. H. R. Fox Bourne. The greater part of the following pages were printed before I faw Mr. Bourne's work. In the laft three chapters it has affifted me to avoid fome inaccuracies, and fupplied a few additions, which are printed in the notes. I am indebted to him for the name of William Wentworth, Burleigh's fon-in-law, referred to (p. 138) in a letter of Sidney's, which, as I should have stated, is taken from Murdin's Burghley Papers, together with those in pp. 135 and 137.

It appears (Bourne, p. 27) that Sidney went to Oxford in his fourteenth year, a year earlier than I have stated on Dr. Zouch's authority. I have been able to prove, from the MS. correspondence of the French Ambassador, the correctness of Mr. Bourne's surmise that Sidney's mission to Paris in 1584 was not carried out, and also to give the reasons why it was revoked: see p. 155.

The dates at which Sidney's works were composed are far more uncertain than would appear from Mr. Bourne's Memoir. In placing them I have partly relied on internal evidence, partly on the opinions of Sidney's editors. The early date 1580, assigned to the " Defence of Poesy," may be sustained by several arguments; the youthful vivacity of the style, the slight, almost apologetic, commendation of Spenser; but more particularly, the appearance, in 1579, of the attack on poetry by Goffon, of which Sidney refufed the dedication: fee p. 65.

Since I have read Mr. Bourne's account of "Aftrophel and Stella," I fee more than ever how arbitrary and infecure is the critical procefs of educing facts from the fcattered verfes of a deceafed poet, efpecially when printed, as thefe were, without fo much as a friendly editor to arrange them. Mr. Collier has fhown, in his Life of Spenfer, lately publifhed, that "Aftrophel and Stella" was printed furreptitioufly by Thomas Nafh, in 1591. The conclufions which I have drawn from Sidney's Poems are fubmitted with diffidence and, as far as poffible, fuftained by direct proofs. Mr. Bourne has fallen into a ferious error as to the date of Lady Penelope Devereux's marriage. The letter on which he relies (p. 286), in correction of the common date 1581, proves his own miftake. I find, by refer- ence to the MS. (Brit. Mus. Lanfdowne MS. xxxi. 40), that he has not taken his ufual care to rectify the year according to the modern calendar, the letter being written on the 10th of March. This error is the more grave that Mr. Bourne's eftimate of Sidney's moral character depends upon it.   Here and there Mr. Bourne has allowed himfelf too great a freedom of paraphrafe.   For inftance (pp. 144, 145), he has put an oration into Sidney's mouth without any fufficient authority.   The words are bafed on Lord Brooke's, who gives the fubftance of Sidney's arguments, not to the Emperor, but to the leffer German Princes, as is evident from an allufion to Auftrian fupremacy (Brooke, p. 50).   Again (p. 343), it is too much to affert that Sidney " determined to retain only fuch parts of" the Arcadia, " as would fit into a ftrictly hiftorical romance, with King Arthur for its hero."   How Sidney would have handled the fable of Arthur is a matter of mere conjecture.   In the familiar anecdote of the wounded foldier Mr. Bourne has deviated capricioufly from his authority, Lord Brooke.   He has altogether omitted to refute or notice the old tradition that Sidney was nominated for the throne of Poland.

The preceding remarks, and fome others which occur in the notes, on Mr. Bourne's Memoir, are rendered neceſſary by the circumſtances under which this volume appears. On the merits and defects of his work in general I ſhall not offer an opinion, further than to acknowledge that the following pages would have gained much if, while they were ſtill in MS, I had been able to avail myſelf of his diligent reſearches.

May, 1862.

CONTENTS.

Contents.

Chapter VII.—Sidney's Death. 1586.

The Life of Sir Philip Sidney.

CHAPTER I.

FAMILY AND CHILDHOOD.

" Kent thy birth-days, and Oxford held thy youth:
  The heavens made hafte, and ftaid nor years nor time :
  The fruits of age grew ripe in thy firft prime,
  Thy will, thy words, thy words, the feals of truth."
SIR WALTER RALEIGH.

THE name of Sir Philip Sidney is one of the brighteft in Englifh hiftory. His fame refts upon the noble title of the praife of thofe who are themfelves moft praifeworthy. Living at an illuftrious period of our annals, his eminent worth as a foldier, ftatefman, and author, was extolled by the general voice of his contemporaries. Such popularity is fometimes a mere fafhion of the day, which is apt to miflead the wifeft judgment, and from which the critics of Elizabeth's reign were

certainly not exempt.   At firſt ſight one might
be inclined to aſcribe Sidney's reputation to this
influence; for the acts of his ſhort career are
hardly ſufficient in themſelves to account for the
applauſe which was beſtowed upon him, and the
univerſal ſorrow of his countrymen when he died.
Yet, although his literary works have long ceaſed
to be popular, few who have written of him in
later times have failed to regard his memory with
admiration almoſt unqualified, and with tenderneſs
reſembling that of private friendſhip.

The ſecret of his fame ſeems to lie in the
ſingular beauty of his life ; which has been well
deſcribed as " poetry put into action."   He was
the perfect type of a gentleman.   If the chief
qualities comprehended under this term are gene-
roſity, dignity, refinement of heart and mind, it
would be hard to find in any age or nation a
better example than Sidney.   His ſoul overflowed
with magnanimity and ſympathy.   Theſe inward
excellencies were ſet off, when living, by extreme beauty of perſon, ſweetneſs of voice, and
proficiency in all accompliſhments and arts, as
well as by a certain gracefulneſs, which appeared
in whatever he did or ſaid, and ſtill ſhines through
his writings with a peculiar charm..

One naturally deſires to meaſure ſo intereſting

a character by the higheſt poſſible ſtandard. To be accounted a perfect gentleman, though it be great praiſe, is far from being the greateſt. Such praiſe is conſiſtent with many defects, and even with ſome of the qualities which are moſt at variance with that Chriſtian holineſs which is the only true ideal of manhood. The indulgence of the paſſions of pride, revenge, and love, is faintly reſtrained by the principle of honour. Still leſs does a man's ſpiritual ſtate, his relation to his Heavenly Father, come within its province. So we find men like Henry IV. of France, reputed the firſt gentleman of his time, and yet undeſerving of any place in Chriſtian biography. How far Sidney may claim ſuch a rank will appear from the following pages. Doubtleſs the career which, from a lower point of view, looks ſo glorious and ſpotleſs, ſhows many traces of error and ſin when we teſt it by the One Perfect Example of Virtue. But Sidney is a man to be brought, without impropriety, to ſuch a compariſon. No vulgar meaſure does him juſtice; and any inſtruction which may be ſuggeſted by his life will beſt ariſe from eſtimating his worth fairly; treating his virtues and accompliſhments as divine gifts, and his faults as examples of the frailty which is common to human nature.

He was born at Penſhurſt, in Kent, on the 29th of November, 1554. His birthplace is one of the chief ornaments of the neighbourhood of Tunbridge Wells: a large old houſe, built in the period when Engliſhmen began to rely on the internal ſecurity of their country, and to diſpenſe with the protection of caſtle walls. Poets have celebrated the beeches and deer of Penſhurſt Park; and an oak, which was ſown at Sir Philip's birth, is famous among Britiſh trees. Ben Jonſon writes, in well-known verſes, of—

> "That taller tree, which of a nut was ſet
>   At his great birth where all the Muſes met."

And on its bark Waller propoſed to commemorate his unrequited love for Philip's great-niece:—

> "Go, boy, and carve this paſſion on the bark
>   Of yonder tree, which ſtands the ſacred mark
>   Of noble Sidney's birth."

An ancient trunk is ſtill ſhown as the Sidney Oak, but the original was cut down a century ago.

The Sidneys came from Anjou in company with Henry II. In the courſe of generations they intermarried with ſome of the nobleſt families in England; and the liſt of their connections includes ſeveral names renowned, in various ways, wherever Engliſh hiſtory or literature is read. It

is fufficient to give, as inftances, the ancient names
of Gray, Talbot, Beauchamp, Berkeley, Lifle;
the great houfes of Pembroke, Stanley, Cavendifh,
Spencer, Brooke ; the refolute defenders of con-
ftitutional liberty, John Hampden and Algernon
Sidney ; the pfalmift George Herbert, and the
poets Byron and Shelley. Sir Henry, the father
of Philip Sidney, was defervedly refpected by
many fovereigns. He was brought up in company with Edward VI, whofe nurfe and governefs
were of Sir Henry's family. Edward often flept
in the fame bed with him, and breathed his laft in
his arms. His firft appointment was that of
henchman to King Henry, whofe three children
in turn employed him in important pofts of ftate.
By Edward he was knighted and fent ambaffador
into France. In Mary's reign he was fent
as Lord Juftice to Ireland, and there, fighting
under the Earl of Suffex againft the northern
rebels, he killed the chief M'Connell with his own
hand. Elizabeth promoted him to the Prefidency
of Wales; and during his tenure of this office,
which lafted for twenty-fix years, he was fent over
to Ireland, as the Queen's Deputy, three times.
In each of thefe vifits he fuftained a violent rebellion, fubdued it, and left the country in quiet.
Ireland was divided by him into counties : he

printed the ſtatutes, and ſet on foot a national
ſcheme of education. His charaƈter was marked
by a grand, manly ingenuouſneſs, not unlike that
of an ancient Roman; but his letters continually betray the warm affeƈtion with which his
ſeverer virtues were tempered.* His wife was no
leſs commended, by thoſe who knew her beſt, for
every womanly virtue and high intelleƈtual gift.
She is deſcribed by her huſband as having been
" a full fair lady, in mine eye at leaſt the faireſt,"
before ſhe loſt her beauty by the ſmall-pox, which
ſhe caught through nurſing the Queen in the
ſame diſeaſe. After that time ſhe lived in much
retirement. This admirable woman was Mary,
eldeſt daughter of the ambitious Duke of Northumberland, and Philip was taught from his
childhood to be proud of his deſcent by the
mother's ſide. " I am a Dudley in blood," he
ſaid in defending his uncle Leiceſter; " my chiefeſt
honour is to be a Dudley." The name is one
of great antiquity, coming from a Saxon chief
Dudo, or Dodo, who built a fort about the
time of the Heptarchy, where Dudley Caſtle

---

* In vol. CLIX. of the State Papers is a moſt intereſting
autobiography of Sir Henry Sidney, written to Walſingham,
for the purpoſe of ſhowing his claim to a penſion.

ftands, encircled by woods, on the edge of the
mines of South Staffordfhire. At the Norman
Conqueft the eftate was given by William to
one of his knights with the hand of the Saxon
heirefs; and from them the Dudleys of a later
date were collaterally defcended. After feveral
generations, marked by no extraordinary diftinction, the family rofe in the fifteenth century
to a high and guilty eminence. Four feveral
Dudleys, in lefs than feventy years, attained for a
time to great power and ftation, from which three
of them fell, ftill more fuddenly, to die on the
fcaffold for high treafon. The firft was Henry
VII.'s minifter, who was brought to trial on the
acceffion of Henry VIII : a bad man, whofe cruel
exactions made him and his family juftly odious
to the people, though he was probably innocent
of the charge on which he was beheaded. His
verfatile fon John Dudley fucceeded, as is well
known, in gaining the favour of Henry VIII.
by his fkill as a foldier and a courtier. He was
made fucceffively Vifcount Lifle, Lord High
Admiral, Earl of Warwick, and Duke of Northumberland; and for a few troubled weeks his
ambition was gratified by hearing his daughter-
in-law ftyled Queen. At the fame time he had
become popular with Ridley and other reformers

by profeffing Proteftant doctrines. The part
which he took in promoting the Reformation is a
ftriking inftance of a good caufe helped, and at
the fame time difhonoured, by the felfifhnefs of a
worldly man. His fall in 1553 feemed to be the
ruin of his family. The death of Guildford
Dudley, on Tower Hill, was the confequence of
his treafon; and his other fons narrowly efcaped
a fimilar fate. John, the eldeft, died in the
Beauchamp Tower, where his infcription, deli-
cately carved, may ftill be feen. Neverthelefs,
in the perfon of Robert, the Dudleys regained
their former eminence. In the face of the taint
of treafon, and of darker fufpicions, which popular
hatred magnified, he lived to be a not unwelcome
fuitor of two rival Queens, and for many years to
exercife, as Earl of Leicefter, a greater influence
on the Englifh State, at home and abroad, than
his grandfather or even his father had ever
poffeffed. Reflecting on thefe wonderful viciffi-
tudes of the houfe of Dudley, there feems to be
at leaft as much caufe for fhame as of pride to one
in whofe veins the fame blood was flowing. If
we grant, as we may, that it is an honour to be
fprung from a noble race, the difhonour of bad
anceftors muft alfo be accepted with humiliation
as our own. But it muft not be forgotten that

the impreſſion which is given in hiſtory of families and individuals is rarely juſt. Hiſtory exaggerates the lights and ſhadows of human character, and more particularly the latter; leaving untold many homely virtues to record one great miſdeed. Thus, among the ſons of Northumberland, the ſecond, Ambroſe, who makes comparatively no ſign in public affairs, was known in his generation as the " good Earl of Warwick."

It was at the time of the loweſt downfall of the family that Philip Sidney was born. The execution of his grandfather, Northumberland, had taken place the previous year, followed by thoſe of his uncle Guildford and of Jane Grey, his aunt by her unhappy marriage. Help came to the Dudleys from the quarter whence it could leaſt have been expected. Philip of Spain, ſolicited by Sir Henry Sidney, and anxious to gain credit in England for clemency, interceded for them, and their forfeited lands and titles were reſtored. Out of gratitude for this favour and loyalty to the Queen, who was married to the Spaniſh King in the ſummer, the infant Sidney received the name of Philip. It has been ſaid that he had Philip for his godfather, but the ſtatement reſts on inſufficient authority. He was the eldeſt ſon of his parents. The children afterwards born to them were two fons, Robert and ~~William~~ Thomas ; and four daughters, of whom three died young, the other being Mary, afterwards Countefs of Pembroke, famous for her learning, beauty, and virtue. Robert Sidney fills a refpectable place in the hiftory of his time, and received the Earldom of Leicefter from James I.

The manners of the family at Penfhurft correfponded with Ben Jonfon's defcription of the next generation of Sidneys :—

> " They are, and have been, taught religion : thence
> Their gentle fpirits have fucked innocence.
> Each morn and even they are taught to pray
> With the whole houfehold ; and may every day
> Read in their virtuous parents' noble parts
> The myfteries of manners, arms, and arts."

On the appointment of Sir Henry Sidney to be Prefident of Wales he went to refide at Ludlow Caftle, and Philip was fent to fchool at Shrewfbury. A long letter which he received from his father in 1556, when he was eleven years old, was carefully preferved, and is extant. In this Sir Henry acknowledges two letters of Philip's, one written in Latin, and the other in French, and he proceeds to give him found advice on the moft important points of duty and behaviour. The letter is indeed a model of its kind. " Let your firſt action," he ſays, " be the lifting up of your mind to Almighty God by hearty prayer, and feelingly digeſt the words you ſpeak in prayer with continual meditation and thinking of Him to whom you pray, and of the matter for which you pray." He counſels Philip to be ſtudious, to be courteous, cheerful, temperate, and cleanly ; to ſtrengthen his body by exerciſe ; to avoid ſcurrilous and ribald converſation ; to be a liſtener rather than a talker : and " above all things," he adds, " tell no untruth, no, not in trifles." He bids him further to ſtudy and endeavour to keep himſelf virtuouſly occupied, and warns him not to diſhonour his noble race ; concluding—" Your loving father, ſo long as you live in the fear of God, H. Sidney." An affectionate poſtſcript follows from his mother :—

" Your noble and careful father hath taken pains (with his own hand) to give you in this his letter ſo wiſe, ſo learned, and moſt requiſite precepts, for you to follow with a diligent and humble thankful mind, as I will not withdraw your eyes from beholding and reverent honouring the ſame, no not ſo long time as to read any letter from me ; and therefore at this time I will write no other letter than this : whereby I firſt bleſs you, with my deſire to God to plant in you His grace :

and fecondarily warn you to have always before the eyes of your mind thofe excellent counfels of my lord your dear father, and that you fail not continually once in four or five days to read them over. And for a final leave-taking for this time, fee that you fhow yourfelf a loving obedient fcholar to your good mafter, and that my lord and I may hear that you profit fo in your learning as thereby you may increafe our loving care of you, and deferve at his hands the continuance of his great joys, to have him often witnefs with his own hand the hope he hath in your well-doing.

" Farewell, my little Philip, and once again, the Lord blefs you ! Your loving Mother,

" MARIE SIDNEY."

From Shrewfbury, Philip went, at the age of fifteen, to Chrift Church, Oxford, where he diftinguifhed himfelf by his love of ftudy and the intelligence with which he maftered what he learned. His tutor was Dr. Thornton, whom he held in grateful remembrance. One of the moft promifing young men of the time, Robert Carew, was felected to difpute with him, according to cuftom, when he took his degree. The difputation took place in the prefence of his uncle, the Earl of Leicefter, who was Chancellor of the

Univerſity. He inherited a delicate conſtitution from his mother, who never recovered from the great ſorrow of her family's overthrow; and he ſeems alſo to have outgrown his ſtrength; for Leiceſter wrote about this time to Archbiſhop Parker requeſting " a licenſe to eat fleſh during Lent, for my boy Philip Sidney, who is ſomewhat ſubjeᶜt to ſickneſs." His weak health inclined him to premature earneſtneſs, though it did not hinder him from ſhowing rare dexterity in manly ſports and exerciſes. The following deſcription of his charaᶜter as a boy is given by his friend and biographer, Lord Brooke:—" Though I lived with him, and knew him from a child, yet I never knew him other than a man, with ſuch a ſtaidneſs of mind, lovely and familiar gravity, as carried grace and reverence above greater years. His talk was ever of knowledge, and his very play tending to enrich his mind." Sidney is ſuppoſed, after leaving Oxford, to have joined Lord Brooke at Cambridge.* His name does not appear on the books of that Univerſity. But it was formerly a common praᶜtice to viſit ſeveral Univerſities, for a ſhort courſe of leᶜtures at each.

A Latin letter is extant among the State

---

* Zouch's Memoirs of Sidney, p. 34.

Papers, in which he gives a diffident account of his ſtudies to Sir William Cecil, better known as the Lord Treaſurer Burleigh. While he was at Oxford a marriage was projected between him and Cecil's daughter Anne. Of this Cecil writes :*—" I have been preſſed with ſuch kind offers of my Lord Deputy, and with the like of my Lord of Leiceſter, as I have accorded with him upon articles, (by a manner of A B without any perſons named,) that if P. S. and A. C. hereafter ſhall like to marry, then ſhall H. S. the father of P. S. make aſſurances, &c.; and then ſhall alſo W. C. the father of A. C. pay, &c. What may follow I know not, but as I wiſh P. S. full liberty, ſo ſurely A. C. ſhall have it, and in the meantime I will omit no point of friendſhip." The contract was never fulfilled, owing, perhaps, to Cecil's ambition ; for Sir Henry Sidney was warmly in its favour. Anne was married young to Edward Vere, Earl of Oxford, whoſe cruelty broke her heart.

---

* Wright's Elizabeth, I. 323.

CHAPTER II.

FOREIGN TRAVEL.

Πολλῶν δ' ἀνθρώπων ἴδεν ἄστεα καὶ νόον ἔγνω.

IN 1572, having completed his academical courfe, Sidney obtained the Queen's licence to travel on the Continent for two years, to learn foreign languages. His retinue, fpecified by the licence, was three fervants and four horfes. Sidney's firft deftination was Paris. He was recommended by Leicefter to the care of Francis Walfingham, the Englifh Ambaffador, and he travelled in the fuite of the Lord Admiral Lincoln, who was fent on an extraordinary miffion to conclude a treaty of alliance with the French King. At that time Paris had begun to take the lead of the European cities in the arts of civilization. The victories which had been gained in Italy by feveral fucceffive kings had eftablifhed the reputation of

French chivalry, and had introduced fouthern taftes and fafhions into France, enriching Paris with choice paintings and ftatues, tapeftry, jewels, and armour, the fpoil of Italian cities. Sidney had the moft favourable opportunities of obferving the mind and manners of the French Court. He was prefented by Walfingham to Charles IX, who treated him with marked kindnefs, and caufed him to be fworn in as one of his gentlemen of the bed-chamber. This, although a poft of honour in a worldly fenfe, was befet with temptations for a youth; and it is not the leaft of Sidney's praifes that he paffed uncorrupted through fuch ex-perience of evil as he muft have acquired at the Louvre. For there, under the mafk of politenefs and of the moft romantic honour, were concealed the vices of men and women without religion, truth, or fhame: poifoners, affaffins, and fome, even in the higheft places, who were devoted to the black art of magic. The feeble King was ruled by his mother, Catherine de' Medicis, who fet the Court an example of cold-blooded iniquity. Paffionlefs herfelf, fhe knew how to make ufe of human paffions, turning to her own account, with Italian craft, the hatred of one, the affection of another, the zeal of a third. But her favourite means of gaining power over the princes and nobles around her was by corrupting and leading their minds with diffolute pleafure. She played with deliberate felfifhnefs the part of a tempter to evil. The chief perfonages in rank after the King and Catherine were her two younger fons, the Dukes of Anjou and Alençon. Of thefe, the former had gained a brilliant reputation in the civil wars, on the fields of Jarnac and Moncontour; but the hopes which he had raifed in his youth were foon difappointed by his effeminate and wicked reign. Francis, Duke of Alençon, fucceeded a few years later to the title of Anjou, on his brother's acceffion to the throne; and a marriage negotiation, which had been commenced with Elizabeth of England on behalf of his brother Henry, was alfo transferred to him. When this marriage was on the point of taking place, and the whole Englifh people was agitated by the profpect, Sidney's former acquaintance with the French Prince and his family gave ftrength to his efforts to diffuade the Queen from alliance with him. He was of a timid and jealous difpofition, and falfe-hearted, though in powers of mind fuperior to his brothers. A ftriking contraft to the fickly members of the royal family of Valois was prefented by the magnificent Henry Duke of Guife, the chief of the Catholic League, and the idol of the populace. He was at the Court, and with him were a multitude of fierce and proud nobles, burning with fcorn of their unworthy princes, and with jealoufy of the minions, Epernon, Joyeufe, and others, who grew rich on their favour. Both thefe two court factions were joined together for the moment in hatred of a third party at the time when Sidney was in Paris. The leaders of the Huguenots were lured to the capital by a feigned peace. It was among the nobleft of thefe, more than among the vain and worthlefs courtiers, that Sidney found his chief friends, men for the moft part older than himfelf, and celebrated throughout Europe for learning and virtue. Philip du Pleffis Mornay, afterwards Chancellor of France, who is reprefented in the Henriade as a guardian angel to his mafter Henry IV, entertained an affection towards Sidney which lafted throughout his life. Another of his friends was Lewis of Naffau, brother of the great William of Orange, and fecond to no one in Chriftendom for combining in himfelf every excellence of knighthood. With the wife Hubert Languet he formed foon afterwards a ftill clofer friendfhip. At the head of this party, which included, befides, Coligni, Condé, and feveral of the moft heroic men in France, ftood the young King of Navarre,

Henry of Bourbon, who was next in fucceffion to the French throne after the King's brothers. He was already eminent for the high perfonal qualities which won for him the crown in fpite of reverfes and obftacles almoft without parallel. Unhappily for his friends and for his fame he became at this time an inftrument of the defigns of Catherine. An aftrologer had predicted to her that all her fons fhould die young and child-lefs, and, though fhe bore Henry no love, fhe gave him her daughter Margaret in marriage, hoping thus to provide for the continuance of her power. The wedding was celebrated at Paris with elabo-rate magnificence in Auguft. A few days later Henry, who was only eighteen years old, was perfuaded or intimidated into renouncing his re-ligion and his party. Meanwhile a plot, which has gained a horrible celebrity, was matured by the Catholic nobles, who feemed intent only on balls and feftivities. On the 24th the city was ftartled by the maffacre of St. Bartholomew.

Sidney efcaped from this great danger by taking refuge in Walfingham's houfe; but itwas evidently unfafe for him to remain at Paris. The perpe-trators of the maffacre were furious men, who only regretted that their work was incomplete, and they were openly encouraged by the King himfelf. So unfcrupulous was the party-fpirit of thofe times in religious queftions, that the Pope was not afhamed to return thanks folemnly at St. Peter's for this great deftruction of the Huguenots, of which even a Roman Catholic bifhop, Perefixe, fpoke freely in the next century as an execrable action of which there had never been the like. At the Englifh Court the utmoft horror and alarm were excited. The ambaffador whom Charles fent to excufe the crime found the Court in mourning, and was received in profound filence.

A letter was immediately written by the Privy Council to Walfingham to take meafures for the departure of Sidney and other Englifhmen from Paris. Under his letter of fafe conduct Philip travelled through Lorraine into Germany, accompanied by Dr. Watfon, afterwards Bifhop of Winchefter. He fpent a fhort time at Strafburg, and from that city went by way of Heidelberg to Frankfort, and took lodgings at the houfe of Andrew Wechel, a printer of fome note. His hoft was, like himfelf, a refugee from Paris, and there was in the fame houfe another refugeè, Languet, who had faved the lives of Mornay and Wechel at his own utmoft peril. Between Languet and Sidney a friendfhip fprang up refembling

that of More and Erafmus. Languet belonged
to an earlier generation. He had been a friend
of Melancthon, and was himfelf eminent as a
Reformer. His learning was thought confiderable in that age of learned men; but he was ftill
more diftinguifhed for his acquaintance with the
ftate of Europe, and for his activity in the
politics of the Proteftant caufe. The charms of
his converfation were extraordinary, and Sidney's
ardent thirft for knowledge was gratified by his
abundant flow of information. Sidney thus com-
memorates his friend in one of the fongs of
Arcadia :—

> " The fong I fang old Languet had me taught,
> Languet, the fhepherd beft fwift Ifter knew;
> For clerkly read, and hating what is naught,
> For faithful heart, clean hands, and mouth as true.
> With his fweet fkill my fkillefs youth he drew,
> To have a feeling tafte of Him who fits
> Beyond the heavens, far more beyond our wits."

When Languet was fent to Vienna, in 1573, as
envoy of the Elector of Saxony, Sidney went
with him, and remained there till the clofe of the
year, taking pains to perfect himfelf in the ufe of
arms and horfemanfhip. The latter he learned
in company with Edward Wotton, brother of the
Sir Henry whofe life Walton has written. His

mafter was an Italian equerry of the Emperor, Pugliano, of great fame in his day, whofe praife of his art is pleafantly defcribed by Sidney. " He faid foldiers were the nobleft eftate of mankind, and horfemen the nobleft of foldiers. . . Then would he add certain praifes, by telling what a peerlefs beaft the horfe was, the only ferviceable courtier, without flattery, the beaft of moft beauty, faithfulnefs, courage, and fuch more, that if I had not been a piece of a logician before I came to him, I think he would have perfuaded me to wifh myfelf a horfe." Sidney made good ufe of his mafter's leffons, and in the fecond book of Arcadia he has admirably defcribed the management of a horfe by a graceful rider.

In the following November, Sidney proceeded into Italy. He refrained unwillingly from vifiting Rome, for he had made a promife to Languet before parting with him that he would not go there. Languet dreaded the impreffion which might be made upon his fufceptible mind by the magnificence of the Papal City; an exceffive caution, perhaps, for it was a vifit to Rome which made Luther a Reformer fixty years before. Yet much had been done in the interval to diminifh the fcandals of the Church: the attractions of St. Peter's had been increafed by many mafter-pieces of art, and the difference was wide between the great German preacher and an imaginative youth of nineteen. Sidney went to Venice, which was in fome refpects a place of more intereft to travellers than Rome. Thofe were the days when Venice was ftill " the revel of the earth, the mafque of Italy." The pompous annual ceremony, in which the Doge committed a wedding-ring to the fea, was fomething beyond an empty boaft, for Venice ftill retained her title to the empire of the fea ; and while the richeft products of Europe and Afia were expofed to fale in her fquares, her pre-eminence as a fchool of arts and manners was not yet eclipfed by the more recent civilization of Paris. Gentlemen of all nations reforted thither, and to float in a gondola through her noifelefs ftreets was reputed to be an effential part of feeing what is called the world. The dramatifts of Queen Elizabeth's reign often take occafion to ridicule the foppery and infolence of young men who had been to Venice. Bifhop Hall, in his youthful fatires, inveighed ftill more earneftly againft thefe and other vices imported from abroad ; and in an effay written later he treats of the fame fubject. Lord Burleigh faid, " Suffer not thy fons to pafs the Alps, for they fhall learn nothing there but pride, blafphemy, and atheifm;" and no language can be ftronger than that which is afcribed to Sidney himfelf, though he wifely confines his ftrictures to the abufe of travel :—

> " An Englifhman that is Italianate
>   Doth lightly prove a devil incarnate."

It is not furprifing that doubts fhould exift whether anything can be gained by travel at all worth the rifk of evil which is incurred. Certainly thofe who vifit foreign countries need to have fixed principles of faith. In that cafe the enlargement of mind which travel gives tends to humility, wifdom, and charity. But if any one has not learned rightly the leffons of his own home, he is not fit to travel yet. Experience of foreign manners fhakes the religion and morals which are founded on mere cuftom, and offers nothing better inftead; its ufe, at the beft, being mainly political. The queftion is difcuffed by Hampden, in a letter to Sir John Eliot, who had confulted him as to the education of his fon. He advifed delay and more ftudy at home before the young man went abroad. " 'Tis a great hazard, methinks," he writes, " to fee fo fweet a difpofi-tion guarded with no more, amongft a people whereof many make it their religion to be fuperftitious in impiety, and their behaviour to be affected in manners. But God hath defigned him (I hope) for his own fervice betimes, and ftirred up your providence to hufband him thus early for great affairs. Then fhall he be fure to find Him in France that Abraham did in Sichem and Jofeph in Egypt, under whofe wing alone is perfect fafety."

Sidney was manifeftly called to "great affairs," both by his birth and by his high qualities of mind; and the true ufe of travel appears nowhere more clearly than in his correfpondence. The following letter was written for the guidance of his brother Robert about five years after this time, but its contents make it fuitable to be cited here.

"My Good Brother,

"You have thought unkindnefs in me that I have not written oftener unto you, and have defired I fhould write unto you fomething of my opinion touching your travel; you being perfuaded my experience thereunto be fomething which I muft needs confefs, but not as you take it; for you think my experience grows from the good things which I have learned; but I know the only experience which I have gotten is to find how much I might have learned, and how much indeed I have miffed, for want of directing my courfe to the right end and by the right means. . . . . I am fure you have imprinted in your mind the fcope and mark you mean by your pains to fhoot at; for if you fhould travel but to travel or to fay you had travelled, certainly you fhould prove a pilgrim to no purpofe. But I prefume fo well of you, that though a great number of us never thought in ourfelves why we went, but a certain tickling humour to do as other men had done, you purpofe, being a gentleman born, to furnifh yourfelf with the knowledge of fuch things as may be ferviceable for your country and calling; which certainly ftands not in the change of air, for the warmeft fun makes not a wife man; no, nor in learning languages, although they be of ferviceable ufe, for words are but words in what language foever they be, and much lefs in that all of us come home full of difguifements, not only of apparel, but of our countenances, as though the credit of a traveller ftood all upon his outfide; but in the right informing your mind with thofe things which are moft notable in thofe places which you come unto.

" Of which as the one kind is fo vain, as I

think ere it be long, like the mountebanks in
Italy, we travellers fhall be made fport of in
comedies; fo may I juftly fay, who rightly
travels with the eye of Ulyffes doth take one of
the moft excellent ways of worldly wifdom.
For hard fure it is to know England without
you know it by comparing it with fome other
country, no more than a man can know the
fwiftnefs of his horfe without feeing him well
matched. . . . . This, therefore, is one notable
ufe of travellers, which ftands in the mind and
correlative knowledge of things, in which kind
comes in the knowledge of all leagues betwixt
prince and prince; the topographical defcription
of each country; how the one lies by fituation
to hurt or help the other; how they are to the
fea, well harboured or not; how ftored with
fhips, how with revenue, how with fortification
and garrifons; how the people, warlike, trained,
or kept under; with many other fuch confidera-
tions, which as they confufedly come into my
mind, fo I, for want of leifure, haftily fet them
down. . . . . . . The other kind of knowledge
is of them which ftand in the things which are in
themfelves either fimply good or fimply bad,
and fo ferve either for a right inftruction or a
fhunning example. Thefe Homer meant in this

verfe, 'Qui multos hominum mores cognovit et urbes.'* For he doth not mean by 'mores' how to look or put off one's cap with a new-found grace, although true behaviour is not to be defpifed: marry my herefy is, that the Englifh behaviour is beft in England and the Italian's in Italy. But 'mores' he takes for that from which moral philofophy is fo called; the certainnefs of true difcerning of men's minds both in virtue, paffions, and vices. And when he fays, 'cognovit urbes,' he means not, if I be not deceived, to have feen towns and marked their buildings; for furely houfes are but houfes in every place: but he attends to their religion, politics, laws, bringing up of children, difcipline both for war and peace, and fuch-like.

" Thefe I take to be of the fecond kind, which are ever worthy to be known for their own fakes. As furely in the great Turk, though we have nothing to do with him, yet his difcipline in war matters is worthy to be known and learned. Nay, even in the kingdom of China, which is almoft as far as the Antipodes from us, their good laws and cuftoms are to be learned; but to

---

* " Wandering from clime to clime obfervant ftrayed,
　　Their manners noted, and their ftates furveyed."—Pope.

know their riches and power is of little purpofe for us, fince that can neither advance nor hinder us. But in our neighbour countries, both thofe things are to be marked, as well the latter as the former. The countries fitteft for both thefe are thofe which you are going into. France is above all other moft needful for us to mark, efpecially in the former kind; next is Spain and the Low Countries; then Germany, which in my opinion excels all others as much in the latter confidera-tion as the other doth in the former; yet neither are void of neither; for as Germany, methinks, doth excel in good laws and well adminiftering of juftice, fo are we likewife to confider in it the many princes with whom we may have league, the places of trade, and means to draw both foldiers and furniture thence in time of need. So on the other fide, as in France and Spain, we are principally to mark how they ftand towards us both in power and inclination; fo are they, not without good and fitting ufe, in the generality of wifdom to be known. As in France the courts of parliament, their fubaltern jurifdiction, and their continual keeping of paid foldiers. In Spain, their good and grave proceedings, their keeping fo many provinces under them and by what manner, with the true points of honour. . . .

Flanders likewife, befides the neighbourhood with us, hath divers things to be learned, efpecially in governing their merchants and other trades. Alfo for Italy, we know not what we have, or can have, to do with them, but to buy their filks and their wines; and as for the other point, except Venice, whofe good laws and cuftoms we can hardly proportion to ourfelves, becaufe they are quite of a contrary government; there is little there but tyrannous oppreffion, and fervile yielding to them that have little or no right over them. And for the men you fhall have there, although indeed fome be excellently learned, yet are they all given to counterfeit learning, as a man fhall learn among them more falfe grounds of things than in any place elfe that I know; for, from a tapfter upwards, they are all difcourfers in certain matters and qualities, as horfemanfhip, weapons, painting, and fuch are better there than in other countries; but for other matters as well if not better you fhall have them in nearer places.

" Now refteth in my memory but this point, which is the chief to you of all others: which is the choice of what men you are to direct yourfelf to; for it is certain no veffel can leave a worfe tafte in the liquor it contains, than a wrong teacher infects an unfkilful hearer with that which hardly will ever out. I will not tell you fome abfurdities I have heard travellers tell : tafte him well before you drink much of his doctrine. And when you have heard it, try well what you have heard before you hold it for a principle ; for one error is the mother of a thoufand. But you may fay, how fhall I get excellent men to take pains to fpeak with me ? Truly, in few words, either by much expenfe or much humblenefs."

Sidney declared to Languet for himfelf, that his chief felicity, next to the worfhip of God, confifted in the friendfhip of good men. He was happy in the poffeffion of fuch a friend, to whom he could look for fympathy and encouragement in his virtuous aims; as he faid of him in the fong already quoted :—

> "His good ftrong ftaff my flippery years upbore,
> He ftill hoped well becaufe I loved truth."

His letters to Languet have a playful ferioufnefs and modefty very becoming in a young man addreffing one fo much his fenior, and the correfpondence between them gives a vivid picture of the "lovely and familiar gravity" which drew all kinds cf men to delight in Sidney's fociety. The tendernefs of his difpofition is agreeably illuftrated by a remark of Languet's. "I am amufed at

your complaints of the ungracious behaviour of
fome friends who went away without bidding you
farewell. You imagine perhaps that all men
have the fame obliging character as yourfelf."

Perfonal matters, however, occupy only a fmall
portion of the correfpondence. Sidney's thoughts
were ftrongly intent on politics, and the ftate of
Europe was fuch as to excite the deepeft anxiety.
The Low Countries were engaged in a feemingly
hopelefs conteft with Spain, and the caufe of the
Reformation throughout Europe hung upon the
iffue. At the fame time Germany and Italy were
menaced by the encroachments of the Turks, who
had lately conquered Cyprus, and concluded peace
with Venice while Sidney was there. Thefe are
the chief fubjects of his letters. When his friend
the gallant Lewis of Naffau was defeated and
killed, he wrote, " If there is any one who fees
what is to follow, and is not moved by it, I fay
he fhould either take his place among the gods,
or be claffed with the brutes in human form."

There is no certain account of Sidney's meeting with any of the illuftrious men of fcience or
letters who were then living in Italy; although it
has been conjectured, with fome probability, that
he may have known Taffo and others. But the
fruits of his having ftudied Italian literature with

delight appear in his Arcadia. He wrote with much intereſt of his ſtudies, which he purſued ‹ for ſome months at the Univerſity of Padua. That univerſity was famous for the expoſition of Ariſtotle's Ethics, as we gather from Shakeſpeare, and Languet recommended this ſtudy to Sidney. He took eſpecial pleaſure in the Politics of the ſame great philoſopher. "Of Greek literature," he told Languet, "I wiſh to learn only ſo much as ſhall ſuffice for the perfect underſtanding of Ariſtotle." Afterwards, however, he learned to love Plato. Hiſtory was at preſent his favourite ſtudy. In one of his letters he alludes to a theory, founded on the language of the Cymry, and comparing curiouſly with the reſearches of modern ſcholars, that Wales was the native country of Brennus, the conqueror of Rome. The advice which he afterwards gave to his brother Robert, doubtleſs founded on his own purſuits at this ſeaſon, contains remarks on ancient hiſtorians which ſhow that he had given to them much thoughtful attention. He alſo urges his brother to "take delight in mathematics." Speaking of Latin ſcholarſhip, he finds fault with the Oxford profeſſors for minding words to the neglect of things; and with a ſimilar downright love of reality he gives his advice about ſword exerciſe.

D

" When you play at weapons, I would have you get thick caps and brafers, and play out your play luftily." In the fame letter he writes, " Sweet brother, take a delight to keep and increafe your mufic; you will not believe what a want I find of it in my melancholy time."

While Sidney was at Venice his portrait was painted by Paul Veronefe. This picture does not appear to exift, and Languet defcribes it as more like his brother. It is poffible that Sidney's features might be found among the groups of noble cavaliers and fquires with which that great artift filled his canvas. His figure was tall and well formed; his hair of a dark amber colour; his face refembling that of his fifter Mary,* fomewhat too feminine if criticifed, but very beautiful. Languet afterwards received another portrait as a prefent from his friend, and of this he fays, " It is fo beautiful, and fo ftrongly re-fembling you that I value nothing more. The painter has reprefented you fad and thoughtful. I fhould have been better pleafed if your face had worn a more cheerful look when you fat for the painting." In truth, he loved Sidney as if he had been his own fon. Exiled from his native

---

* An excellent portrait of the Countefs of Pembroke is in the National Collection.

country France, where he had loſt all his kindred
and his deareſt friends in the civil wars and in the
fatal maſſacre, the whole affection of his lonely
life was centred upon the young Engliſhman
whom Providence had ſent in his way to cheer
his declining years. His letters to Sidney were
long and frequent, and he was contented to receive
occaſional replies.

After a ſojourn of eight months in Venice and
Padua, Sidney left Italy in the ſummer of 1574,
and paſſed through Germany rapidly on a viſit
to Poland. The throne of that kingdom was
then vacant. Henry of Valois, the Duke of
Anjou, had been elected king the year before,
after a long interregnum ; but he had ſcarcely
arrived from Paris when he received intelligence
of the death of his brother Charles IX, by which
he ſucceeded to the French crown. He deſerted
his ſubjects without delay, ſtealing by night from
the caſtle of Cracow, and leaving the kingdom in
confuſion. But his eagerneſs to return to France
did not prevent him from lingering at Venice,
where he was entertained ſumptuouſly while
Sidney was there. It was immediately afterwards that Sidney travelled through Poland, the
condition of which was full of intereſt for ſo inquiring a ſtudent of politics. He had an oppor-

tunity of obferving that which he defcribes in his
romance with great force of language as the worft
kind of oligarchy—the arbitrary government of
nobles in the interval between two reigns.   By
the good offices of Languet he had introductions
to fome Poles of high rank; and it is afferted, with
fome probability, that he took part in a campaign
againft the Mufcovites, and gained there his firft
experience of war.*   The mad Ivan, furnamed
the Terrible, was then upon the Ruffian throne,
and had much to do to preferve his independence
between his more powerful neighbours the Poles
and Tartars.

Sidney's travels led him into Hungary, where
he noted with admiration the foldier-like bearing
of the people, and their cuftom at feafts and
fimilar affemblies of finging heroic ballads of
their anceftors' valour.   There were Hungarians
ftill living who had fought under Lewis, the laft
of their native kings, at the calamitous battle of
Mohacz, when the flower of their youth and
knighthood was cut off by the Turks, and an
incredible number of captives fold into flavery.
The kingdom had been devaftated again and
again by invafion, fince it had been joined to the
other inheritances of the houfe of Auftria.   And

---

* Aubrey, quoted by Pears, xlviii.

although the laſt of the great Moſlems, Soly-
man the Magnificent, was dead, and the ſpring-
tide of their conqueſts had begun to ſubſide, the
Sultan's arms continued for many generations to
be a terror to the German empire. Sidney had
thought of viſiting Conſtantinople to inſpect the
ſources of this formidable military power. But
his leave of abſence was already expired; and,
whether for this or for other reaſons, he gave up
the project.

During the winter he enjoyed again the ſociety
of Languet at Vienna ; and in May of the following year he returned to England. He had ex-
ceeded by twelve months the term for which his
original permiſſion to travel was granted. The
profeſſed object of his tour, to learn foreign
languages, was attained indifferently well : he
could read French, Italian, Spaniſh, and Dutch,
and had ſtudied German a little, though he never
ſucceeded in maſtering the pronunciation. He
had thus acquired enough to juſtify his ſubſe-
quent reputation at the Engliſh Court as a lin-
guiſt; for Latin being a univerſal means of com-
munication, the ſtudy of modern languages was
rare. But he had made far greater proficiency
in acquirements of a more valuable kind, having
gained a wonderful ſtore of knowledge, both of
men and books, for his age : a judgment ſcarcely

lefs found than that of an experienced ftatefman: and a power, fuch as few men ever poffefs, of apprehending the firft principles of every fubject, whether it pertained to religion, politics, philofophy, or tafte. Nor did he lefs excel in the graceful arts and exercifes of youth. Among the accomplifhed gentlemen who furrounded the throne of Elizabeth, he was at once obferved by the quick eye of his Sovereign and diftinguifhed by her favour. She called him " her Philip," in contraft to Philip of Spain.

Little is known of his life for the next year, during which his time was apparently paffed chiefly at Court. In the autumn of 1576 he made a journey to Ireland, whither his father had gone as Lord Deputy. Languet expreffed an anxious fear of the perils of his journey acrofs " the rugged Welfh mountains and the ftormy Irifh fea." The Irifh were in arms againft the Government, and Philip, during this vifit to his + father, faw fome fervice in the North under the Earl of Effex ; of which, however, the particulars are not recorded.* Before the end of the year he came back from Ireland to the Court.

---

* G. Whetftone's poem in Sir Alexander Bofwell's collection. In the Sidney Papers, feveral letters of the year 1576-7 have been mifplaced.

Early in 1577 his fifter Mary was married to Henry, Earl of Pembroke, fon of the Earl who had commanded the Englifh army in Flanders, and himfelf, as was afterwards proved, a wife and valiant nobleman, one of the foremoft to volunteer in defence of England on the approach of the Armada, when he equipped 300 horfe and 500 foot at his own expenfe. Writing on the fubjeĉt of this marriage to Leicefter, in February, Sir Henry fays, " Good my Lord, fend Philip to me ; there was never father had more need of his fon than I have of him. Once again, good my Lord, let me have him." He was difappointed of his fon's vifit by a caufe which in other refpeĉts muft have gladdened his heart.

A fpecial embaffy was fent in this fpring to Rodolph, Emperor of Germany, on his acceffion, and Philip was feleĉted for ambaffador. The charge was one of unufual refponfibility ; for while his oftenfible commiffion was to condole with the young Emperor on his father's death, he was inftruĉted to found the German princes in reference to the great queftions of religion and policy which divided Europe. Among the heads of his inftruĉtions are thefe : to afcertain the new Emperor's difpofition and that of his brothers ; by whofe advice he is guided ; when he is likely to marry; what princes in Germany are moft favourably difpofed to him; what the ftate of his revenue is; how he agrees with his brothers, and what portion they have. He was alfo directed to pay a fimilar vifit of condolence and diplomacy to the Counts Palatine of the Rhine, who had lately loft their father. An article was added, at his own inftance, by which he had leave to falute at his difcretion thofe Princes who might be interefted in the caufe of the Reformed Religion, or contending for their national liberty. He was only in his twenty-third year when thefe important charges were laid upon him. His appointment was due to the Queen's perfonal efteem, though it may probably have been in fome meafure promoted by the influence of Leicefter, who had recently entertained the Queen with the celebrated revels of Kenilworth. The choice was fignally juftified by Sidney's conduct. In thofe days men feem to have attained to maturity more early in life than at prefent. Sidney's father, for inftance, had been fent at the fame age as ambaffador to France. William of Orange had commanded the Imperial army when ftill younger. Don John of Auftria, at the age of twenty-fix, had gained the great victory of Lepanto over the Turks, at the head of the united navy of

Chriſtendom. The rarity of ſuch caſes in our time is eaſily explained. The circle of knowledge is wider, ſo that ſchool education extends over a greater number of years. In the peaceful ſtate of modern ſociety there are fewer emergencies of difficulty and danger, in which ſelf-reliance is chiefly acquired. The opportunities of diſtinction are fewer, for the ſame cauſe; and while under a more equal conſtitution merit has now a ſurer proſpect of being recognized in the end, there is leſs room for favour or high rank to ſecond the advantage of brilliant talents by bringing them early into notice.

Sidney ſeems to have endeavoured, with ſome little oſtentation, to impreſs foreign nations with his dignity; if anything may be inferred from the fact which has been thought worth recording, that he cauſed his arms and titles to be emblazoned on a ſhield and ſuſpended outſide his lodgings wherever he reſted on his journey. Through life he was fond of ſplendour to a fault, and there may have been ſomething unuſual in manner which cauſed ſo trifling a circumſtance to be chronicled. But in negotiations his behaviour was peculiarly ſimple and unaffected. He truſted to the inherent power of plain truth to a degree which is not uſual in diplomacy. Of this his interview with the Elector Palatine is an inftance. He found him differing from his brother, Prince Cafimir, on fome of the theological queftions which already rent the union of the Proteftants, and changing the form of worfhip which his father had eftablifhed, to introduce Lutheran minifters. Thereupon Sidney ventured to warn him unrefervedly of the confequences which might follow. " One thing I was bold to add in my fpeech," he reports to the Secretary of State; " to defire him, in her Majefty's name, to have merciful confideration for the Church of the religion fo notably eftablifhed by his father, as in all Germany there is not fuch a number of excellent learned men, and truly would rue any man to fee the defolation of them. I laid before him as well as I could the dangers of the mightieft princes in Chriftendom by entering into like violent changes, the wrong he fhould do his worthy father utterly to abolifh what he had inftituted, and fo as it were condemn him, befides the example he fhould give his pofterity to handle him the like."

He found the Emperor at Prague, and had audience with him on Eafter Monday. According to the commands which he received, he exprefled the Queen's grief at the lofs of the late

Emperor his father, both for public reafons and for the private goodwill between Maximilian and herfelf; adding her Majefty's hope that he would follow his father in his virtues and his manner of government, and further explaining to him the Queen's policy in the Netherlands. Rodolph anfwered briefly in Latin, giving her "Serenity" very great thanks, and affuring her of his knowledge of the goodwill which his father had borne towards her. To the latter part of the Queen's meffage he replied vaguely, faying, however, that the rule he fhould chiefly follow would be his father's imitation.

"The next day," Sidney writes, "I delivered her Majefty's letters to the Emprefs, with the fingular fignification of her Majefty's great goodwill to her, and her Majefty's wifhing of her to advife her fon to a wife and peaceable government. Of the Emperor deceafed I ufed but few words, becaufe in truth I faw it bred fome trouble unto her to hear him mentioned in that kind. She anfwered me with many courteous fpeeches, and great acknowledging of her own beholdingnefs to her Majefty: and for her fon, fhe faid, fhe hoped he would do well, but that for her own part fhe had given herfelf from the world, and would not

greatly ftir from thenceforward in it.   Then did
I deliver the Queen of France * her letter, fhe
ftanding by the Emprefs, ufing fuch fpeeches as
I thought were fit for her double forrow, and her
Majefty's goodwill unto her, confirmed by her
wife and noble governing of herfelf in the time
of her being in France.   Her anfwer was full of
humblenefs, but fhe fpake fo low that I could not
underftand many of her words.   From them I
went to the young Princes, and paffed on each
fide certain compliments."

He proceeded to inform himfelf of the particulars contained in his inftructions, of which he
wrote a full report in the fame letter to Walfingham, who was now Secretary of State.   His
opinion of the young Emperor was on the whole
unfavourable.   He defcribes him as very Spanifh
in appearance and manners, ftrongly inclined to
wars, few of words, fullen of difpofition, very
fecret and refolute, deficient in his power of winning friends, though conftant in keeping them.
This minute defcription of Rodolph's character,
in which Sidney was doubtlefs aided by the
penetration and knowledge of Languet, proved

---

* The widow of Charles IX, a daughter of the Emperor
Maximilian.

in the main correct, but his acts showed no signs
of his warlike difpofition. He neglected public
affairs, and fpent his time in his ftables or in his
laboratory, leaving the adminiftration of his kingdom and empire to bigoted Catholics.

From Prague Sidney returned to Heidelberg,
where he had the interview with the Elector
Palatine Lewis which has been already related.
The Elector's brother Cafimir had previoufly
become acquainted with Sidney, who had paffed
through Heidelberg on his way to the Imperial
Court. They continued faft friends through life.
He was one of the moft zealous Proteftant
champions, an active leader in the civil wars
both of France and the Netherlands ; and Sidney
was inftructed to demand of him the repayment
of a loan which Elizabeth had made him on
account of thefe. Cafimir, the Duke of Brunf-
wick, and the Landgrave William of Heffe are
named by Sidney as the only princes who were
likely to enter into any Proteftant league, and
even they " rather as it were to ferve the Queen
than any way elfe." Of the other German princes
he faid that they had " no care but how to grow
rich and to pleafe their fenfes, thinking they fhould
be fafe though the world were on fire about them."
Already the zeal of the Reformed Churches was

cooling or expending itself in sectarian contro-
versies. In Bohemia Sidney found indifference
to the liberty of public worship; in Saxony, persecution of Lutherans by Calvinists; in the Pala-
tinate, persecution of Calvinists by Lutherans.
Meanwhile the Catholics regained their strength;
and thus the course of the Reformation in Germany receded, until, in the next generation, the
Thirty Years' War overspread the whole empire
with misery and ruin.

Sidney came home through the Netherlands.
At Brussels he went to kiss the hand of the newly
appointed Viceroy, Don John of Austria. This
Prince had filled Europe with the fame of his
romantic daring; and though as yet he was at
peace with Elizabeth, it was rumoured that he
would before long marry Mary Queen of Scots,
conquer England, and restore the Roman Catholic
religion. He regarded himself as a Crusader
against Turks and Protestants alike. So he received
Sidney, when he was first presented to him, with
more than Spanish haughtiness. After a while,
however, he was so much attracted by Sidney's
brilliant qualities as to pay him a degree of respect
and honour which astonished those who knew his
disposition.

With Don John's great antagonist Sidney became acquainted immediately afterwards; for, by the Queen's special orders, he proceeded to Holland.* It had been his own earnest desire to visit William of Orange, "Father William," as he was called by the Dutch, who owed to him, under God, the blessings of religious and civil freedom. Of the many friends by whose esteem Sidney was honoured, the Prince of Orange may justly be regarded as the greatest. Love of his country had led him to sacrifice his prosperity and happiness in a contest the most desperate and most glorious, perhaps, recorded in history; and the trials of manifold calamity and innumerable cares, while fortifying his resolute soul against human weakness, taught him, with increasing years, to put his trust in Heaven with more fervent devotion and purer faith. His outward appearance showed the change which his mind had undergone. Formerly he had been conspicuous among the sumptuous nobles of Belgium for luxury and courtly refinement; but for many years his thoughts and his ample fortune had been absorbed in the conflict with Spain; and a short time after Sidney's visit, Lord Brooke saw him at Delft, in a gown " such as an English law-student

---

* Languet, Correspondence, 1577.

would be afhamed to wear," and a knit woollen waiftcoat like that of a waterman. The burgeffes of that town were his affociates, among whom he appeared as no more than their equal; though his inward greatnefs manifefted itfelf as foon as he began to fpeak to his vifitor. On that occafion he told Lord Brooke, as a meffage from himfelf to the Queen, that "he had been acquainted, as was well known, with all the greateft men of Europe for many years, and that if he could judge, her Majefty had one of the ripeft counfellors of ftate in Sir Philip Sidney that this day lived in Europe; on which he ftaked his credit, till her Majefty might be pleafed to employ him." The meffage remained undelivered, by Sidney's own requeft; for he judged prudently that a commendation coming from abroad might neither advance his interefts nor pleafe the Queen. In this vifit of Sidney to the Prince of Orange, he is faid to have become fponfor to his child.* The Princefs gave him on his departure a gold chain and jewel, and William afterwards corresponded with him familiarly.

His opinions on the ftate of Europe bear traces of the Prince's influence on his mind. According

---

* Letter of E. Waterhoufe in Sidney Papers, June, 1577.

to William, the Spanifh king aimed at reviving the univerfal empire of ancient Rome, and for the fake of the Pope's alliance feigned religion. France, ruled by a fucceffion of young and plea-fure-feeking princes, was of little weight in Europe; and Elizabeth was to blame for fuffer-ing the Proteftants in that kingdom to fail for want of fupport, and altogether not enough upon her guard againft the arts of Philip. Germany was a blind inftrument of the Spanifh tyrant's plans. Upon this general view of the policy of Europe Elizabeth acted at length, after many years of hefitation, during which Sidney fupported it conftantly through favour and disfavour.

He returned from his embaffy in June. Wal-fingham immediately wrote to Sir Henry to announce the Queen's approval of his fon's con-duct in his difficult miffion. " It was," he faid, " well received and liked of her Majefty;" and he added, " The honourable opinion he hath left behind him, with all the princes with whom he had to negotiate, hath left a moft fweet favour and grateful remembrance of his name in thofe parts. . . . There hath not been any gentleman, I am fure, thefe many years, who hath gone through fo honourable a charge with as great commendation as he. In confideration whereof

E

I could not but communicate this part of my joy with your Lordfhip." He ufed afterwards to fay that Philip far overfhot him with his own bow, though he had an influence in all countries, and a hand in all affairs. Another correfpondent defcribed his embaffy as profperous in every refpect. "God bleffed him fo, that neither man, boy, nor horfe failed him or was fick during this journey; only Fulke Greville had an ague in his return at Rochefter." To the affection of this conftant friend and companion, afterwards Lord Brooke, and anceftor of the prefent Earl of Warwick, we owe the beft part of what is known of Sidney. They were both admitted on the fame day to Shrewfbury fchool, and were intimate affociates through life. The love which Fulke Greville bore to Sidney was little fhort of worfhip. After outliving him half a century he caufed this epitaph to be infcribed on his own tomb, which may be feen in St Mary's Church at Warwick :—

> Servant to Q. Elizabeth,
> Counfellor to K. James,
> and Friend to Sir Philip Sidney.
> Trophæum Peccati.

The fenfe of the laft words is obfcure, but may probably be thus interpreted : an honourable friendſhip is a trophy which holds up one's own faults to reproof. A ſimilar ſentiment is ex-preſſed in " In Memoriam :"—

> " All theſe have been, and thee mine eyes
> Have look'd on : if they look'd in vain,
> My ſhame is greater who remain,
> Nor let thy wiſdom make me wiſe."

Chapter III.

COURT OF QUEEN ELIZABETH.

"In one thing only failing of the beſt,
That he was not ſo happy as the reſt."

SPENSER'S *Aſtrophel*.

IT will not be altogether ſuperfluous to recall a few particulars of the ſtate of England when Sidney took his rank among her worthies. Looking back with juſt veneration to that heroic time, we are apt to confound the greatneſs of the men with the condition of the kingdom, and to imagine the England of Elizabeth as far more powerful, populous, and flouriſhing than it really was. For ſecurity of perſon and property, and for the comforts of ſocial life, the remote parts of Ireland or the colonies are now at leaſt as far advanced in civilization; and ſingle counties exceed in population and reſources the whole realm of Elizabeth.

At that time, moreover, Scotland, inſtead of adding to the national ſtrength, was a dangerous rival kingdom. Ireland, though nominally ſub-ject, was in armed rebellion under native chiefs, whoſe determined courage exerciſed all the wiſdom and energy of Sir Henry Sidney, foiled two Earls of Eſſex, and only yielded to the ſkill of Mount-joy in the year of Elizabeth's death. Nothing remained of the rich provinces of France which had belonged to earlier Britiſh ſovereigns; Calais, the laſt poſſeſſion, having in the preceding reign fallen an eaſy capture to the Duke of Guiſe. On the other hand, the vaſt colonial empire of Great Britain had not yet begun. The firſt ſucceſsful attempts at colonization were made in the reign of James, for previous expeditions ſerved only for diſcovery and knowledge hardly won by failure. Internally, England was weak-ened by religious diviſions ſimilar to thoſe which convulſed the reſt of Europe. Though happily the Queen's able government, and her adherence in general to the principles of the Reformation, preſerved the kingdom from civil war, ſhe was menaced by more than one formidable riſing, and her life was in danger from conſtant plots of the Papiſts for her aſſaſſination. How terrible was the mere apprehenſion of this event may be inferred from a letter of the Bifhop of London on the occafion of the maffacre at Paris, urging the minifters to behead the Queen of Scots without delay as a precaution for public fafety.* Another determined adverfary to the Crown was flowly rifing in the faction of the Puritans, who began to threaten the Conftitution with republican theories of Church and State which they had learned from Geneva. As yet, however, the great body of the nation was bound together by the common fear of the Pope and the King of Spain. Minor differences were compofed by the dreadful remembrance of the fires of Smithfield, and the more recent and fweeping atrocities of the Duke of Alva in the Netherlands. But befides the uncertainty of the fucceffion and the horror of Papal and Spanifh tyranny, other caufes confirmed the loyalty of the Englifh to their Proteftant fovereign, fo that it grew to be a kind of religion.

The extraordinary worfhip which Elizabeth received was very characteriftic of that epoch. It was the age of tranfition from the days of chivalry to thofe of regular government. The refpect for women which belonged to the former, and had been their fhield againft lawlefs violence,

---

* Letters publifhed by Sir H. Ellis.

continued in full vigour ſtill as a ſentiment: but
women no longer ſtood in need of ſuch protection; and knights who were ambitious to prove
their gallantry were driven to ſeek adventures
which did not readily offer themſelves. Extravagant feats of courage and fantaſtic devotion
had become a faſhion both in England and
France; and in Spain their prevalence is ſtill
more notorious from the ridicule which was caſt
upon them in the Romance of Don Quixote.

Thus, as a Maiden Queen, the only one who
had ever reigned over any nation known in hiſtory,
Elizabeth was a peculiar objeƈt of reverence to the
knighthood and gentry of England. If this had
been all, her popularity might have been limited
to the upper claſſes of ſociety; but the maſs of
the nation was diſpoſed to revere the Queen for
another reaſon, which acquired from aſſociation a
certain degree of ſacredneſs. The Royal ſupre-
macy was the moſt tangible point at iſſue with
the Pope, to the multitude who had not learning
nor inclination for deep queſtions of theology.
The ſtrong national deſire, expreſſed by the words
of Shakeſpeare,—

> "That no Italian prieſt
> Shall tithe or toll in our dominion,"

had grown to be almoſt univerſal ſince the reign

of Mary, and had attached to the Reformation many lukewarm Chriftians who had beftowed no ferious thought on the principles of faving faith which were involved. The ill-taught populace faw for the moft part with regret the images of their faints caft down in the churches, and miffed the obfervance of their feftivals. It would be unreafonable to fuppofe that the idolatrous wor-fhip of human excellence fhould on a fudden have been altogether extinguifhed when the old idols were fwept away; but one form which it affumed is curious, and could fcarcely have been anti-cipated. Saint worfhip paffed over into hero worfhip.

Comparing the writers of Elizabeth's time with our own, we cannot but obferve the fulfome praife which it was cuftomary to lavifh on eminent men whether diftinguifhed by virtue, genius, or courage. We at the prefent day are fo much inclined to the oppofite extreme of irreverent criticifm, that we find it hard to underftand how honeft and rational men could ufe fuch language as was common, efpecially in fpeaking of the Queen. The truth appears to be that a habit of veneration, originally directed to Roman Catholic faints, continued for a while after the removal of its objects; and Elizabeth ftrangely fucceeded in a qualified degree to the idolatry of the Virgin Queen of Heaven. Mary has always been regarded by Catholics as in fome fenfe the Church perfonified. Elizabeth claimed for herfelf the title of Head of the Church, to which long ufe had given a myfterious and awful import.* Nor is it an infignificant circumftance that Proteftants applied to Elizabeth the vifion in the Apocalypfe, of the woman whom the great Dragon perfecuted. For that myftical woman, crowned with ftars and clothed with the fun, had been for centuries a familiar image of Mary, and an object of adoration.

Thus Faith and Chivalry combined to inveft Elizabeth with attributes borrowed from the fading fuperftitions of each; and her temperament led her to make the moft of thefe advantages. Her appetite for praife was boundlefs; no adulation was too profane or too coarfe to gratify her; while her wifdom faw the importance of winning and preferving the popular goodwill

---

*   " Not choice
But habit rules the unreflecting herd,
And airy bands are hardeft to difown :
Hence, with the fpiritual fovereignty transferred
Unto itfelf, the Crown affumes a voice
Of recklefs maftery, hitherto unknown."
                                        WORDSWORTH.

which was the only sure support of her throne. The imperiousness with which she exercised her authority, in the government both of the State and of the Church, may fairly be called tyrannical. Yet she was not altogether unworthy of her glory. Her high and resolute spirit extorted the unwilling admiration of her bitterest enemies, and the hearts of her people thrilled at the words in which she defied the greatest king and the greatest captain of the time. Her feminine weaknesses were so far restrained by prudence that they never lost her the love or respect of her subjects. Though fond of dress and magnificence, she was frugal; and her partialities were balanced by a careful regard to the public service and to the advice of wise counsellors. Neither Leicester nor Essex gained that ascendancy in the government which James and Charles permitted to their favourites. Her surprising discernment also saved her preferences from the blame of folly. For instance, when her handsome captain of the guard, Sir Christopher Hatton, was made Lord Chancellor, the lawyers were furious; but in a short time he not only won general esteem by his urbanity and industry, but showed legal abilities which no one had suspected.

A natural refult of the Queen's influence and character was that perfonal rivalries were mixed up with politics undifguifedly. In the highflown ftyle of the Court, Elizabeth's prefence was the fun, and to feek her goodwill was to feek light and warmth which were neceffary to life. The moft approved warriors and ftatefmen were obliged to become courtiers, and to enlift in their fervice every art which could delight the mind or the eye. Beauty of face and figure, tafte and fplendour in apparel, fkill in the tournament or in the dance, and, not leaft, a happy turn of flattery, were as ferviceable as real worth in bringing into notice the fortunate afpirant; and if, like Raleigh, he had folid qualities befides thofe which were on the furface, his voice was foon liftened to when the affairs of Europe were debated, whatever might have been his rank or parentage. England was overflowing with generous enthufiafm, heroic enterprife, and widely-ranging ambition, of all which Elizabeth's court was the centre. Among the hoft of young men that were attracted thither Sidney had every title to diftinction, and the Queen received him after his return from Germany with higher favour than before. She made him her cupbearer, an office which was not without refponfibility or peril of poifon; and fhe alfo gave him a lock of her hair.* On New Year's Day it was her cuftom to interchange prefents with many of the gentlemen and ladies of her Court. In fome lifts of thefe which have been preferved Sidney's name appears firft among the efquires who received the Queen's gifts, which were always of gold plate.† The prefents which he made in return were various. In 1578 he gave her "a fmock of cambric edged with gold lace;" in 1579, "a waiftcoat of white farcenet, quilted and embroidered with gold and filver and filk of various colours;" in 1580, "a cup of cryftal with a cover;" in 1583, "a jewel of gold, like a caftle, garnifhed with fmall diamonds on the one fide, being a pot to fet flowers in." Elizabeth conferred on him among other penfions a finecure in Wales which was afterwards given to George Herbert by James I.

Sidney took his honours without bafe ambition or vanity. He did not feek the high ftation which feemed to be within his reach. The influence which royal favour and his own talents gave him was employed for the welfare of his country, for

---

* This is preferved at Wilton with fome verfes of Sidney's.
† Nicholls : Progreffes of Queen Elizabeth.

the vindication of his friends, for the patronage of deferving men of every kind. For thefe ends he was willing to forego his private advancement. Nor did he choofe to practife the falfe and fervile adulation towards Elizabeth which fhe exacted as a right. So far, indeed, as courtefy required, he complied with the prevailing fafhion, as appears in the Mafque which he wrote for the Queen's entertainment at Wanftead. Yet his love of truth and manly courage led him to utter his mind with a fincerity which, while it commanded and retained her efteem, left her felf-love diffatisfied. While others gave themfelves up to win favour in her eyes, Sidney preferred to pay his court where honours more genuine and more enduring were to be won. He became known not in England only, but throughout Europe, as the friend of men of letters. Poets, fcholars, muficians, engineers, navigators, hiftorians, thronged his houfe to receive affiftance from his open purfe, and encouragement from his enthufiafm, which was ever ready to be kindled by any noble idea. His London refidence was the houfe of Leicefter, near where Temple Bar now ftands; and his profpective inheritance of the Earl's eftates, as well as thofe of his other childlefs uncle, the Earl of Warwick, added confiderable value to his

patronage.   But the fupport which he gave by
his name and money was made doubly precious
by his fine tafte and ftill more exquifite delicacy
of feeling.   The dedications which he received
were almoft innumerable.*   The great fcholar
Henry Stephens infcribed a work to him; and
fent him a copy of the Greek Teftament, with a
tenderly affectionate letter.   Dr. Powell, the
author of a Hiftory of Wales, addreffed his book
to Sidney, exhorting him to thank God for his
good gifts, and ufe them to the glory of God and
to his country's benefit.   Other books dedicated
to him were Hakluyt's firft volume of Voyages,
the Poetica Geographia of Lambert Dané, the
firft Englifh Tranflation of Taffo, a verfion of a
Spanifh Treatife on the Art of War, and a work
by Theophilus Banco, on the Logic of Ramus,
which was the favourite ftudy of Sidney's friend
and fecretary William Temple, and engaged the
thoughts of learned men much till it was fuper-
feded by the bolder theories of Defcartes and the
philofophy of Bacon.

One of Sidney's friends, Giordano Bruno, has
obtained an unenviable celebrity. He was burnt

---

* Dr. Zouch has given a copious lift of thefe at the end of
his Life of Sidney.

by the Inquifition for a book which he had dedicated to Sidney, and his memory was branded
with the name of Atheift. It was a common art
of the Papifts to ftigmatize thus any one whofe
fpeculations difturbed their eafe or their bigotry,
and Bruno was one of the leaft cautious among
the philofophical inquirers of whom the age was
rife. The nominal offence for which he was
brought to the ftake feems to have been that he
held the theory of the plurality of worlds, which
has fince found orthodox advocates. His real
crime was that he derided the fables of the
Church of Rome.

Pofterity owes a deep obligation to Sidney
in refpect of Edmund Spenfer. He was the firft
to recognize the rare poetical powers of the author
of the Faery Queen. He invited him to Penfhurft, and in friendly converfations encouraged
the bafhful poet to unfold the treafures of his
rich and beautiful mind. There, perhaps, Spenfer
compofed his Shepherd's Calendar, which he
dedicated to Sidney :—

> " Go, little book, thyfelf prefent,
>   A child whofe parent is unkent,
>   To him who is the Prefident
>   Of noblenefs and chivalry."

Sidney is generally fuppofed to have introduced

him to Leicefter, by whom he was brought to the notice of Elizabeth.

There is a popular tale that Spenfer, while yet in obfcurity, fent a portion of the Faery Queen to Sidney, who was fo much delighted with it that he promifed the author 50*l.* for the firft ftanza, and as much more for the next, until the fum amounted to 200*l.*, when he ordered his fteward to pay the poet at once, and fend him away, left he fhould ruin himfelf by reading more. Tradition fpecifies the powerful defcription of the Cave of Defpair, in the ninth Canto of the firft Book, ftanzas 33 to 36. In itfelf the anecdote is improbable in a high degree; but fuch fables are not altogether valuelefs as illuftrating common opinion; and this one difplays, while it exaggerates, Sidney's common repute for liberality and for warm admiration of Spenfer. Another tradition, relating to the fame part of Spenfer's poem, is more likely to be true; that the author intended to portray Sidney in his character of Prince Arthur. There is alfo fome ground for fuppofing that the plan of the poem may have been originally fuggefted by Sidney.

A fingle exception to Sidney's univerfal favour to men of letters only puts his geniality in a more pleafing light. One Stephen Goffon wrote an attack on poets and poetry, and prefumed to dedicate his book to Sidney, for which he was, as Spenfer relates, "fcorned: if at leaft it be in the goodnefs of that nature to fcorn."

At the fame time Sidney was himfelf acquiring fame as a poet. His verfes, though only circulated in manufcript, were much read and praifed about the Court, and his fayings were in every one's mouth. His father, in a letter to Robert Sidney foon after Philip's return from Germany, writes thus: "Follow the direction of your moft loving brother: imitate his virtues, ftudies, and actions; he is a rare ornament of this age, the very formular that all well-difpofed young gentlemen of our Court do form their manners and life by. . . . . . In truth, I fpeak it without flattery of him or of myfelf, he hath the moft rare virtues that ever I found in any man."

In the particulars of Sidney's life there are more inftances than one in which he is to be blamed. There would be fome excufe for treating thefe faults lightly; for in no refpect did he belie his renown as a true-hearted gentleman. They might almoft be paffed over in filence without difingenuoufnefs. Yet both virtue and truth are too holy to be mifreprefented for the fake of any one's fame, and the higheft examples are in

favour of fetting down fairly in a good man's life
his errors and fhortcomings.   The fins of Sidney
are outbreaks of a vehement foul, frank and
generous even in its exceffes, and tempered with
a hearty love of virtue ; fuch fins as few men
would live without committing, and many would
repeat without fcruple : fuch fins, neverthelefs,
as fhould be. remembered with fhame, as thefe
were by Sidney.   Refentment, paffionate love and
pride, emotions which no law, but only the Spirit
of Chrift, can govern, overcame him under
circumftances of extraordinary provocation.   As
far as his actions are concerned he paffed through
thefe temptations blamelefs, but neither in thought
nor in word was he innocent.

Immediately on his return to England he became involved in party conteft on his father's
account.   Sir Henry Sidney's government in
Ireland had been affailed by a ftrong faction at
home, and Philip was compelled to decline Prince
Cafimir's invitation to join the army of the Netherlands, for fear that his father's caufe fhould fuffer
by his abfence.   " I ftrive between honour and
neceffity," wrote Sir Henry.   " If you think not
my matters of that weight and difficulty, but that
they may well enough by myfelf or fome other
without your affiftance be brought to an honour-

able end, I will not be againft your determination."
A new form of land-tax, which had been impofed
by Sir Henry on the Englifh Pale, led indirectly
to feveral acrimonious difputes. The Earl of
Ormond, whofe intereft at the Court was great,
having obtained from the Queen the exemption
of his property, Sir Henry remonftrated againft
this partiality as a great and juft caufe of difcontent
to others. His expoftulations were coldly received,
and he began to hear rumours that he was about
to be recalled. He complained indignantly to the
Queen,—" When I look into the fervice that I
have done, the care and travail that I have taken,
and the found confcience I bear that I have ferved
you faithfully, truly, and profitably, I cannot but
lament with forrow of heart and grief of mind to
receive fuch fharp and bitter letters from your
Majefty; which fo much have perplexed me in
body and mind fince I received them, as I fhall
find no comfort till your Majefty be fully informed and thoroughly fatisfied how I have been
mifreported to you; and they that fo have informed you receive the juft reward of their un-
truths." Political matters were conducted with
fo much fecrefy that he was not able to afcertain
who were his enemies, but he naturally fufpected
the Earl of Ormond. Philip entertained the fame

fufpicion.   His dutiful affection led him to take his father's part with warmth; and the more fo as he believed him to have been foully wronged. On one occafion Ormond fpoke to him at Court, and he remained filent with marked intention. The expectation of a quarrel caufed fome excitement in the Court at Oatlands; but the Earl faid " he would accept no quarrel from a young gentleman that is bound by nature to defend his father's caufes, and who is by nature furnifhed with fo many virtues as he knew Mr. Philip to be."   Philip was touched by his magnanimity, and they were foon afterwards reconciled.

A more ferious incident is connected with the fame affairs.   Sir Henry Sidney's defpatches were communicated, as he thought, to his enemies. Whatever meffages paffed between his fon and himfelf became known to them.   The perfon upon whom Philip's fufpicion fell was Molyneux, Sir Henry's fecretary; to whom he wrote the following violent letter:—

"MR. MOLYNEUX,

" FEW words are beft.   My letters to my father have come to the eyes of fome; neither can I condemn any but you for it.   If it be fo, you have played the very knave with me; and fo I will make you know if I have good proof of it. But that for fo much as is paſt. For that is to come, I aſſure you before God, that if ever I know you to do as much as read any letter I write to my father, without his commandment, or my con- fent, I will thruſt my dagger into you. And truſt to it, for I ſpeak it in earneſt. In the meantime, farewell. From Court, this laſt of May, 1578, by me,

" PHILIP SIDNEY."

Molyneux's reply is a temperate and dignified defence of himſelf againſt this fuſpicion, which feems to have been groundleſs. He remained for many years in the fervice of the family; and Philip had occaſion to folicit his intereſt in Ireland on behalf of Lord Brooke and of himſelf. An eloquent and affectionate memoir of Sir Henry, Lady Mary, and Philip, which is appended to Holinſhed's Chronicle, is from the pen of Moly- neux.

Sir Henry Sidney was recalled in the fame year, 1578, much to the regret of the Iriſh, whom he had ruled with great moderation and equity, but to his own joy; for he looked upon his re- fidence in Ireland as an exile; and as he was fail- ing homeward, he applied to himſelf the Pſalm,

" When Israel came out of Egypt, and the house of Jacob from among a strange people."[*] His immediate successor was Sir William Drury, who was followed, in 1580, by Lord Arthur Grey of Wilton, the Artegall of Spenser's poem.

Previously to these events, the affairs of Ireland had bred another trouble, which brought lasting sorrow to Philip. He was affianced to Lady Penelope Devereux, daughter of Walter, Earl of Essex, before he went as Ambassador to Vienna. Probably the match was on both sides contracted by the parents without reference to the persons chiefly concerned; for Penelope was almost a child, and Philip did not entertain at that time any strong affection for her. In September, 1576, the Earl of Essex died. In his last illness he spoke much of Philip Sidney, who hurried to Dublin to see him, but too late.[†] His death was sudden; and a rumour arose that he had been poisoned by Leicester. Sir Henry Sidney caused an inquiry to be made, which led to no conclusive result. Essex's death was caused, without doubt, by Leicester's double dealing; though it may be questioned whether he was guilty of the

---

[*] Moore: History of Ireland.
[†] State Papers, MS. vol. clix.

odious charge which was generally whifpered, and confirmed in popular opinion by his fecret marriage with Effex's widow foon afterwards. The deceafed earl was a devout Chriftian, a gallant foldier, and exemplary in every relation of life. His difpofition was of that guilelefs kind which is goaded into fury by craft in others ; and he had been rendered miferable by Leicefter both in his own home and in his Irifh campaigns. It had been the wifh of his heart that his daughter Penelope fhould marry Philip Sidney, whom he took plea-fure in calling, by anticipation, his fon. Whether for political or for perfonal reafons, Sir Henry cooled towards the project ; and after Effex's death fhowed fome difpofition to break it off : but he feems to have been hindered by the high refpect in which all men held the memory of Effex. When Philip returned from Holland, in 1577, Penelope Devereux was growing into womanhood. Soon he began to difcover in her every grace of mind and perfon. She was by common confent very lovely and witty ; of a character not unlike her brother Robert's, fubject to noble impulfes of affection and generofity, but unftable. The end of her life, equally with his, though in a different way, was fad and fhame-ful. In her youth, however, fhe feems to have been worthy of Sidney's love. Gradually his admiration for her grew to a paffionate affection. In his own words :—

> " Not at firft fight, nor with a dribbed fhot,
> Love gave the wound which, while I breathe, will bleed ;
> But known worth did in mine of time proceed,
> Till by degrees it had full conqueft got." *

But now various obftacles interpofed, and he bitterly regretted his loft opportunity :—

> " I might, unhappy word! O me! I might,
> And then would not, or could not, fee my blifs." †

His profpects were blighted by the birth of a fon to Leicefter in 1579. At a tilt foon afterwards Philip changed the motto upon his fhield, *Spero*, to *Speravi*, croffed out. For he was no longer his uncle's heir ; and Lady Leicefter, a felfifh and vulgar-minded woman, defired a more ambitious match for Penelope than a mere efquire. Befides, the Sidneys were not rich. Their princely ftate and liberality had kept their fortune fo low that Sir Henry was reduced to afk Leicefter for 2000 crowns as a portion for his daughter Mary. Lady Penelope was, however, ftill young, and remained unmarried for two years more. Her

---

* Sonnet II.   † Sonnet XXXIII.

refidence at Leicefter Houfe brought her into intimate familiarity with Philip, and he perfifted in cherifhing his love with an ardour which was to fharpen his future defpair.

It is ftrange that Shakefpeare's editors have overlooked the parallel between the plot of Hamlet and the circumftances which were affociated by popular fufpicion with the death of Effex. Sidney's likenefs has more than once been traced in the words of Ophelia :—

> " The courtier's, fcholar's, foldier's, eye, tongue, fword,
> The expectancy and rofe of the fair ftate,
> The glafs of fafhion, and the mould of form,
> The obferved of all obfervers."

A clofer analogy between Sidney and the Prince of Denmark feems to have been unfufpected. Yet we have before us, in the preceding incidents, the very outline of Hamlet, and originals of the chief characters. The beginning of Sidney's griefs was the death of his adopted father under the fufpicion of poifon adminiftered by his uncle, who married the widow with indecent hafte, fimilar to that which is defcribed in the play :—

> " The funeral baked meats
> Did coldly furnifh forth the marriage tables."

Both Shakefpeare and his audience would certainly be reminded of fo notorious a fcandal by the old Danifh tale which he chofe for the foundation of his tragedy. The earlieft notices of a play of Hamlet occur about the time of Leicefter's death, and within a few years of the appearance of the libel which has chiefly given publicity to this charge againft him. Sidney, it is true, had no doubt of his uncle's innocence. The parallel cannot be preffed into detail without confounding the effential .differences of poetry and hiftory; though feveral curious counterparts may be obferved, efpecially Horatio and Languet. But Sidney's writings certainly exhibit a phafe of brooding irrefolution in his life. This tranfient phafe Shakefpeare feems to have caught, and elaborated into the moft profound and finifhed of all types of charaćter, ufing fuch incidents as would beft develope his own idea. The conjećture will not appear extravagant if Hamlet be confidered in his brighter afpećts, not only as diftrażted with melancholy, but as the accomplifhed fwordfman, the patron and critic of the players, the brilliant wit, the gallant champion, made prifoner alone through his forwardnefs.* Sidney's felf-reproach is thoroughly in Hamlet's ftrain :——

---

* It has been fuppofed, not without probability, that the famous allegorical fpeech of Oberon, in " Midfummer Night's

" My youth doth wafte, my knowledge brings forth toys,
 My wit doth ftrive thofe paffions to defend
Which for reward fpoil it with vain annoys.
 I fee, my courfe to lofe myfelf doth bend ;
I fee, and yet no greater forrow take
Than that I lofe no more for Stella's fake." *

While he was thus abforbed in his own affection the expected marriage of the Queen became a matter of anxiety to the whole nation. Numerous fuitors had been propofed for Elizabeth ; among whom Sidney's friend, Prince Cafimir, offered himfelf, with flight hope of fuccefs. He came, notwithftanding, to England in Jan. 1579, and brought in his fuite Languet, who undertook the journey for the purpofe of feeing Sidney once more, and was rejoiced to hear his praifes from the Queen's own lips. Some difappointment, however, mingled with Languet's pleafure: he would rather have feen Sidney fighting in the ranks of the Proteftant heroes on the Continent. " It was a delight to me laft winter," he wrote, " to fee you high in favour and enjoying the efteem of all your countrymen ; but, to fpeak plainly, the habits of your Court feemed to me fomewhat lefs manly than I could have wifhed ; and moft of your noblemen appeared to me to

---

Dream," has a covert allufion to Leicefter's marriage with Lady Eflex. See Craik's Romance of the Peerage, 1. 74.
 * Sonnet XVIII.

feek for a reputation more by a <u>kind of affected</u> <u>courtefy</u> than by thofe virtues which are whole-fome to the State, and which are moft becoming to generous fpirits, and to men of high birth.   I was forry, therefore, and fo were other friends of yours, to fee you wafting the flower of your life on fuch things; and I feared left that noble na-ture of yours fhould be dulled." Sidney was aroufed by the project of an alliance between Elizabeth and Francis Duke of Anjou, which had been in treaty for many years, and now was affuming the form of an engagement.   Public and private motives confpired to recommend this marriage to the Queen, and Burleigh, after a careful balance of oppofing arguments, decided in its favour.   The policy of an union between England and France, to counteract the over-whelming power of Spain, was very apparent. In France there was good reafon to believe that the great faction of the League was in corre-fpondence with Philip II, whofe earneft defire to regain the kingdom of England, by any means, was well known.   The war in the Netherlands afforded moft alarming proofs of the fkill of his generals, and of the courage and difcipline of his army; while their fuccefs was likely to encourage them to greater enterprifes.

Hence Elizabeth had been fearful of breaking with France. She had forborne to refent the perfecution of the Huguenots, and even the great crime of St. Bartholomew's day did not interrupt the alliance; though many of her ftatefmen, and Sidney among them, advocated a bolder policy. He often faid that " our true-heartednefs to the Reformed Religion brought peace, and fafety, and freedom to us." Temporifing, he faid, was falfe both to God and man, and likely to be forfaken of both. But the Queen liftened more willingly to the counfellors who, like Burleigh, recommended caution. There was no prince then unmarried whofe alliance gave fo much promife of defence againft Philip of Spain as Anjou. Not only was he brother to the King of France, but in 1578 he was invited by the revolted Provinces of the Netherlands to bring a French army to their defence. In cafe of his fuccefs, Elizabeth had to provide for the fecurity of Englifh and Proteftant interefts. To Anjou, on the other hand, it was ftill more important to gain the co-operation of England in his enterprife.

Perfonally, alfo, the Queen was inclined towards the marriage. The French prince, though ill-made and plain-featured, was not unattractive. He was proficient in his national art of flattering without feeming to flatter; and Elizabeth was at this time more than ufually fenfible of her lonely ftate, being deeply offended with Leicefter. His fecret marriage, difcovered to her by the French Ambaffador, if the common ftory may be believed, made her fo angry that fhe threatened to fend him to the Tower. She was not only indignant at the fcandal, but jealous; for, though fhe did not herfelf choofe to marry him, fhe was willing to receive from him the homage of a fuitor, and his exclufive devotion gratified her. The wife whom Leicefter had chofen was obnoxious to her, with good reafon; and though fhe foon reftored him to favour, and fanctioned by her prefence the public celebration of his wedding,* fhe could no longer rely on him with the fame confidence as before. It is probable that this incident difpofed her to accept an offer of marriage from Anjou. Leicefter, as was natural, oppofed the project vehemently. The Englifh people in general difliked it; but it was perilous to exprefs an opinion contrary to the Queen's will. Stubbs, a barrifter, who wrote a pamphlet entitled, "The Gulph in which England will be fwallowed by the French Marriage," was condemned to lofe his right hand:

---

* Sept. 1578. Nicholls: Progreffes.

a fentence which he bore with memorable fortitude, waving his cap with the other, and crying,
" Long live Queen Befs !" Neverthelefs, Sidney
ventured to lay before the Queen with great
plainnefs the dangers which the marriage threatened to herfelf and to her people. Having already declared his opinion to Elizabeth by word
of mouth, he addreffed to her, in the winter of
1579,* a letter, remarkable for its courage, and
no lefs for its wifdom and eloquence. His au-
dacity was juftified to his own confcience by his
being urged to this ftep by " fome whom he was
bound to obey," as he informed Languet; but he
took the whole refponfibility upon himfelf.

This famous letter is addreffed, " Moft feared
and beloved, moft fweet and gracious Sovereign ;"
and he enters without apology upon his fubject :
" Carrying no other olive branch of interceffion
than the laying of myfelf at your feet, ... I
will, in fimple and direct terms, (as hoping they
fhall only come to your merciful eyes,) fet down
the overflowing of my mind in this moft important matter, importing, as I think, the con-

---

* Commonly dated 1580 ; but Languet's correfpondence
fhows it muft have been written before the beginning of the
year.

tinuance of your fafety ; and, as I know, the joys of my life."

England, he faid, was divided into two great parties. The Proteftants, to whom fhe had granted the free exercife of the eternal truth, and who were her chief, if not her fole ftrength, would be galled to fee her "take for a hufband a Frenchman and Papift, in whom the very common people well know this, that he is the fon of the Jezebel of our age ;" and himfelf, no lefs than his brother, a treacherous perfecutor of the Huguenots. The other party, the Papifts, he defcribes as malcontent, doubtful of Elizabeth's title to the throne, numerous, rich, united, and wanting only a head, which they would have in Anjou. Of the Prince's ambition and ficklenefs Sidney fpeaks with little referve, giving reafons for apprehenfion that he might bring French troops into England, and reminding the Queen of "his inconftant temper towards his brother, his thrufting himfelf into the Low Country matters, his fometimes feeking the King of Spain's daughter, fometimes your Majefty." Glancing at the bad faith of the family, he fays, "I will temper my fpeeches from any other unreverend difgracings of him, (though they might be never fo true)." Yet a little further on he contrafts him thus with Elizabeth, as ill-matched together—" he embracing all ambitious hopes, having Alexander's image in his head, but perhaps ill-painted : your Majefty, with excellent virtue, taught what you fhould hope; and by no lefs wifdom, what you may hope."

" Often," he urges, " have I heard you with proteftation fay, that no private pleafure nor felf-affection could lead you to it;" and he combats her alleged motives : the fear of ftanding alone in refpect of foreign dealings, and contempt in thofe from whom fhe fhould have refpect. Denying that fhe fuffers any injury from thefe caufes, he reminds her how odious her fifter Mary's marriage with a ftranger had been to the people, and concludes his argument thus :—" For your ftanding alone, you muft take it for a fingular honour God hath done you, to be indeed the only protector of His Church. Againft contempt, if there be any, which I will never believe ; let your excellent virtues of piety, juftice, and liberality, daily, if it be poffible, more and more fhine." " Not to be evil fpoken of, neither Chrift's holinefs nor Cæfar's might could ever prevent or warrant ; there being for that no other rule than fo to do as they may not juftly fay evil of you."

The effects of this letter did not appear immediately. For three years the marriage continued to be impending, though the Queen was eventually perfuaded to break off the engagement. Her prolonged hefitation is afcribed in part to Sidney's remonftrances, which fhe pondered often and anxioufly. She forgave the boldnefs of fpeech which he had ufed; but his opinions brought to him fome lofs of favour. Contrary to his own intention, the letter became known,* which difpleafed the Queen, and incenfed againft him the party which was inclined to the French alliance.

Of this party the Earl of Oxford was one of the moft influential. He had married Lord Burleigh's daughter Anne, the fame who in her childhood had been contracted to Sidney. He delighted the Queen by his accomplifhments, and ftill more by his prefents of embroidered gloves, and other new inventions which he brought from Italy. His affectation of foreign manners made him an object of popular ridicule; but his talents were various and brilliant. He received from Elizabeth the prize at a tournament about this time, when Sidney was one of the four challengers with him. As a poet he had a reputation which lives to the prefent day, and the lateft anthologies include fome of his verfes. His ability as a ftatef-

---

* Languet's Correfp.

man was alfo confiderable. To thefe qualifica-
tions he added a family name among the nobleft
in Europe, high rank, and a rich eftate which he
had not yet fpent. His morals, however, were
bad, and his temper overbearing. Sidney, about
the time that his letter was written, was playing
tennis in the court of the palace, when Oxford
entered, and infolently bade him make room
for him; on which Sidney anfwered, that, " if
his lordfhip had been pleafed to exprefs defire in
milder charaders, perchance he might have led
out thofe that he fhould find would not be driven
out." The Earl retorted by calling Sidney a
puppy. Unfortunately the French ambaffadors
had audience that day, and being in the private
galleries which overlooked the tennis-court of
Whitehall, preffed to the windows to fee and enjoy
the quarrel. Sidney, obferving this, and feeling
himfelf to be in the prefence of many enemies,
grew warmer, and demanded of the Earl in a loud
voice what he had faid; Oxford thereupon repeated the infult, and Sidney rejoined by giving
him the lie direct, which was not to be miftaken
by the punctilious as a provocation to a duel.
With a few more angry words, Sidney quitted
the tennis-court, unwilling to make the Queen's
palace the fcene of a brawl, or to lower the dig-

nity of his nation in the prefence of foreigners. His departure was mifconftrued by the Earl, who proceeded to his game, with little advantage, as was thought, to his reputation. Having waited in fufpenfe for a day, expecting a challenge from Oxford, Sidney fent a friend " to awake him out of his trance."*

A duel had not yet loft its ancient fignificance as analogous in nature to a court of juftice. Thus Sidney, a few years afterwards, defied the anonymous libeller of his uncle; offering to " prove upon" his body the untruth of his charges. There was probably no one in Queen Elizabeth's Court who would have fcrupled to give or accept a challenge, or queftion the morality of duelling any more than that of war. Inafmuch as Sidney was high-principled and thoughtful beyond others, he deferves fome meafure of blame for complying with an unchriftian fafhion. But it is never fair to cenfure a man by the ftandard of a later age. There is a flow and fitful progrefs in the morals of the world, and when we look back through hiftory to the names which are affociated with moft eminent virtue, we find their excellence depending mainly upon greatnefs or purity of heart,

* Brooke.

not on exemption from the common faults of their contemporaries. Languet wrote to Sidney, " I am aware that by a habit inveterate in all Chriſtendom a gentleman is diſgraced if he does not reſent ſuch an inſult, but ſtill I think you were unfortunate to be drawn into this contention, though I ſee that no blame is to be attached to you for it."* He conſidered, however, that Sidney went further than he ought, after retorting the inſult offered to him by giving the lie, in being the challenger.† Prince Caſimir ſent word to Sidney, expreſſing his ſympathy and his willingneſs to aſſiſt him. Sidney himſelf wrote to Hatton :— " As for the matter depending between the Earl of Oxford and me, certainly, ſir, howſoever I might have forgiven him, I ſhould never have forgiven myſelf, if I had lain under ſo proud an injury as he would have laid upon me ; neither can anything under the ſun make me repent it, nor any miſery make me go one half word back from it. Let him, therefore, as he will, digeſt it. For my part, I think tying up makes ſome things ſeem fiercer than they would be."‡

* Pears' Sidney's Correſp.

† Lord Hailes' Langueti Epiſtolæ : a paſſage not inſerted in Pears.

‡ Wright's Elizabeth, ii. 101. ·

Oxford hefitated long between pride and anger : thinking it beneath his dignity to fight a duel with a commoner; and fo much time elapfed that the Lords of the Council interfered and tried to make peace. Failing in their attempts, they appealed to the Queen, who undertook to fettle the matter herfelf. She accordingly fent for Sidney, and laid before him "the difference in degree between earls and gentlemen, the refpect inferiors owed to their fuperiors, and the neceffity in princes to maintain their own creations, as the degrees defcending between the people's licentioufnefs and the anointed fovereignty of crowns; how the gentleman's neglect of the nobility taught the peafant to infult upon both."

Sidney replied firmly, vindicating himfelf by arguments, the independence of which was foftened by characteriftic grace in the manner of ftating them. "That place was never intended for privilege to wrong," he urged from her own example; who, as he faid, "how fovereign foever fhe were by throne, birth, education, and nature, yet was fhe content to caft her own affections into the fame mould as her fubjects did, and to govern by their laws." He befought Elizabeth to remember that Oxford, "though a great lord, was no lord over him; and therefore the difference of degrees among freemen could not challenge any other homage than precedency." He also appealed to her prudence, inftancing the policy of her father Henry VIII, who thought it wife by upholding the gentry to guard the throne againft the ambition of the grandees.

It was afterwards ftated that Oxford fent Raleigh and another gentleman to Sidney, propofing an honourable agreement, that Sidney had acceded, but that Oxford's overtures were a cloak for a plot to murder Sidney in his bed. This accufation proceeds apparently from a bitter enemy of the Earl.*

Shortly after this, Sidney retired for a time from the Court. This ftep has been afcribed to his unwillingnefs to make an apology for a wrong in which he was the injured party. But it appears from Languet's correfpondence that he was chiefly induced to withdraw himfelf by the prevailing influence of Anjou and the French faction. "I admire your courage," Languet writes, Jan. 30, 1580; but at the fame time he cautions Sidney againft going too far in incurring unpopularity, and againft being angry becaufe the advice which

---

* State Papers, vol. CLI: Depofitions of Lord Henry Howard and Charles Arundel, MS. 1581.

he gave was not received as it deſerved.   But Sidney was greatly diſappointed at the ſtate of public affairs, and quitted the Court for Wilton, the ſeat of his dearly loved ſiſter, the Counteſs of Pembroke.

CHAPTER IV.

ARCADIA.

> " I love to cope him in thefe fullen fits,
>   For then he's full of matter."
> *As You Like It.*

OR fome time before Sidney left the Court he had begun to figh for a purer life than he found there. Among his earlieft effays in verfe is a tranfla-tion of Horace's Ode in praife of an intermediate courfe between ambition and bafenefs :—

> " The golden mean who loves, lives fafely free . . .
>   Releafed from Court, where envy needs muft be."

The laft line, expreffing with added energy the fenfe of the original, fhows the temper of his own mind. His thoughts turned towards the country, and contrafted with a penfive fancy the fimple ways of nature with the perverfenefs of the world of fafhion. " O fweet confolation !" he writes, " to fee the long life of the hurtlefs trees! to fee how in ftraight growing up, though never fo high, they hinder not their fellows! They only envioufly trouble, which are crookedly bent."

A little poem of his, entitled, " Difpraife of a Courtly Life," defcribes himfelf in the character of a fhepherd, lamenting his change to the ftate of a courtier :—

> " Well was I, while under fhade
> Oaten reeds me mufic made,
> Striving with my mates in fong,
> Mixing mirth our fongs among ;
> Greater was the fhepherd's treafure,
> Than this falfe, fine, courtly pleafure.
>
> *   *   *   *   *   *
>
> My old·mates I grieve to fee,
> Void of me in field to be,
> Where we once our lovely fheep,
> Lovingly, like friends did keep ;
> Oft each other's friendfhip proving,
> Never ftriving, but in loving."

Among his numerous friends he fingles two, who had not difappointed him, and whom he entreated to make with himfelf " one mind in bodies three :"—

> " Only for my two loves' fake,
> In whofe love I pleafure take ;
> Only two do me delight
> With their ever-pleafing fight."

Thefe were Fulke Greville and Edward Dyer, both of them poets, to whom Sidney afterwards bequeathed the whole of his books.

His hopeful and imaginative mind had formed much too fair an idea of the world, and he was difgufted in proportion with the reality; yet he perfifted in cherifhing the conception of a ftate, in fome other place and period, in which the virtues flourifhed which he had not found in England or in Italy. During the leifure which he enjoyed in his retirement at Wilton he amufed himfelf by delineating his ideal ftate, a kingdom where every knightly excellence flourifhed in combination with the unfophifticated manners of a rural life. The place which he felected was Arcadia, in the remote times of the Meffenian wars; and as his fiction was written down for the pleafure of his fifter, he called it the Countefs of Pembroke's Arcadia. In a letter to her he compares it to a fpider's web, fit only to be fwept away: the fruit " of a young head full of fancies, and not fo well ftayed as I would it were, and fhall be when God will. It is done for you," he fays, "only for you; not for feverer eyes, being only a trifle, and triflingly handled. Your dear felf can beft witnefs the manner, being done on loofe fheets of paper, moftly in your prefence: the reft by fheets

sent unto you as fast as they were done." The
earlier and more finished part was written in the
Earl of Pembroke's stately mansion of Wilton,
then newly built from the designs of Holbein.
A fire and many alterations have left only a small
portion of the original house standing; and some
paintings from the Arcadia, with which one of the
apartments was adorned, have long been oblite-
rated. But in the park there is still an ilex under
which Sidney may have sat, as he is depicted in
Isaac Oliver's portrait, musing with folded arms.
There, before his eyes, rose the glory of English
cathedrals, the unrivalled spire of Salisbury; and
sometimes in riding over Salisbury plain he would
roam among the huge blocks of Stonehenge, wonder who had piled them, and compare them to the
shapeless fancies which encumbered his mind.
John Aubrey, whose great-uncle had seen Sir Philip,
describes him as taking a pocket-book with him
in his rides, and often pausing to set down thoughts
which struck him.* His delight in a country life
seems rather to have been such a taste as town-
bred men are wont to have, than the mere love
of rural sports and scenes for their own sake.
Natural beauty was chiefly delightful to him as

---

* Gray.

an image of moral beauty; and his mind reverted continually from meadows and trees to human interefts. He defcribes his Arcadians as "a happy people, wanting little, becaufe they defire not much;" yet their difcourfe is almoft entirely of things which belong to civil life, and that of a refined kind; of kingdoms, wars, tournaments; of courtly paftimes and fentimental love. Whether fuch a ftate be poffible, as he imagines, with all that is pure in ruftic innocence, and all that is noble in political virtue, or graceful in art and knowledge, may well be doubted; but the contemplation of fuch a ftate is at leaft a beautiful dream.

A fimilar idea had been conceived previoufly by Spanifh and Italian authors; and Sidney had read both the Diana of Montemayor and the Arcadia of Sannazzaro. Of the former, indeed, he tranflated fome portions. But the hints which he certainly borrowed from thofe once popular romances he has worked out in a manner of his own, and his work is diftinguifhed by his peculiar reflectivenefs. At the prefent day few would think of Sidney's Arcadia otherwife than as a tedious book. Fafhions change in fiction almoft as much as in drefs, fo that what was the admiration of one age appears to another the height of abfurdity and deformity. Only thofe poems en-

dure in freſhneſs which render a true image of the
eternal properties of nature, and more eſpecially
of the human ſoul. Many other compoſitions.
little inferior in genius have become antiquated,
becauſe they have been loaded with conceits peculiar to one age.

The mixture of adventurous chivalry and feudal
courteſy with affected worſhip of the gods of Greece,
in which Sidney's proſe-poem abounds, paſſed
during a ſhort time for the union of all perfections.
As long as the taſte prevailed of blending claſſical
and mediæval ideas, no book was more admired.
Thirteen editions were printed in leſs than a
century, a number which was not attained even
by Lyly's popular Euphues; and it was thought
worth while to caution young wives againſt waſt-
ing their time over the Arcadia to the neglect of
their houſehold duties. But both of the two
elements which contributed moſt to its popularity
have grown out of date. The ſpirit of chivalry
faded away from England in the ſecond generation after Sidney, and has only of late years been
reſtored to literature in an hiſtorical form, chiefly
as a contraſt to modern democracy. The imagery
of ancient gods and goddeſſes paſſed more gradually out of faſhion. In the ſixteenth century it
was in the bloom of freſhneſs, and was far from

being really fo profane as it might feem. For a
great change of mind took place at the revival of
learning and art in reference to the ancient my-
thologies. The primitive Chriftians had regarded
the heathen Pantheon as a Pandemonium. The
gods of Greece and Rome were to them evil fpirits,
devils who refifted Chrift and deceived his people.
Far otherwife did they appear to the great fcholars
who after a thoufand years difinterred the old
claffical world: for them the fame deities, ftripped
of their religious awe and antagonifm to the Chriftian faith, had only their firft and pureft attributes.
Formerly they had been identified with the rebel
angels; now they feemed like angels who had never
rebelled. Pan, the god of Nature, Pallas, the
goddefs of Wifdom, Diana, the goddefs of Chaftity,
and the reft, were conceived as fo many minifter-
ing fpirits attending upon thofe feveral depart-
ments of God's kingdom. In this fuperftition, as
in the faint-worfhip to which it fucceeded, there
lurked, without doubt, the germ of idolatry, which
in the next century degenerated into a mere ornament of irreligion. But in its origin it was promoted by a defire to claim for Jehovah fupreme
dominion over all things vifible and invifible;
and it was fuftained by a reverent wifh to avoid
the familiar ufe of His Name.

One inftance will fhow how much earneftnefs there was in this incongruous mixture of deities. A princefs in the Arcadia is reprefented as uttering in prifon a prayer, which is quoted at length. This prayer was ufed at Carifbrook by Charles I, and given by him to Juxon at his death. It is printed in " Eikon Bafilike," under the title of " A Prayer in Time of Captivity." Milton, in his pamphlet " Iconoclaftes," rebukes the king fharply for adopting the prayer, both as being a plagiarifm from Sir Philip Sidney, and as a heathen prayer. Yet it is impoffible to read it without acknowledging its appropriatenefs to the circumftances of Charles ; and his ufe of it, rather than a fault in him, is an honour to Sidney, who has imbued a pagan romance with fo Chriftian a fpirit.*
On the whole, however, Milton's character of the Arcadia, though too fevere, is not far from a juft eftimate. He calls it, in the fame paffage to which reference has been made, " a vain amatorious poem, a book in that kind full of worth and wit; but among religious thoughts and duties not

---

* The intereft which is attached to this prayer feems a fufficient reafon for inferting it at the end of this volume, as Arcadia has been long out of print. Milton has been abfurdly accufed of procuring the infertion of the prayer in order to ftigmatize it.

worthy to be named, nor to be read at any time without good caution." Sidney himfelf, when on his deathbed, wifhed it to be deftroyed. Like other compofitions of the fame kind, it is replete with the worfhip of youth, beauty, and martial excellence. In magnifying the qualities of heroes and heroines, many voluptuous and fanguinary pictures are drawn, which are not altogether redeemed by their affociation with high fentiments and examples. Yet the glowing fancies of fuch men as Sidney have fometimes a wholefome influence to which ethical treatifes never attain. Reaching minds which from felf-indulgence have come to loathe other teaching, they excite an admiration for manly virtues which are equally valuable as a preparation and as a fupplement to higher Chriftian graces. The following fententious extracts would perhaps be of little value, if they were thruft into a frivolous book in order to give it a mere colour of gravity. Some may eafily be referred to claffical fources; others are trite with fubfequent ufe: yet they deferve notice as they flow out of the courfe of the romance, and reprefent fairly the fpirit in which it is conceived:—

" Wifdom and virtue are the only deftinies appointed to man to follow."

H

" There is no man fuddenly either excellently good or extremely evil, but grows either as he holds himfelf up in virtue, or lets himfelf flide to vicioufnefs."

" True love hath that excellent nature in it, that it doth transform the very effence of the lover into the thing loved; uniting and as it were incorporating it with a fecret and inward working. And herein do other kinds of loves imitate the excellent; for as the love of heaven makes one heavenly, the love of virtue virtuous; fo doth the love of the world make one become worldly, and the effeminate love of a woman doth womanize a man."

" They are never alone who are accompanied with noble thoughts."

" Who fhoots at the midday fun, though he be fure he fhall never hit the mark; yet as fure he is, he fhall fhoot higher than who aims but at a bufh."

" High honour is not only gotten and born with pain and danger, but muft be nurfed with the like, or elfe vanifheth as foon as it appears to the world."

" If we will be men, the reafonable part of our foul is to have abfolute commandment; againft which if any fenfual weaknefs arife, we are to yield all our found forces to the overthrowing of fo unnatural a rebellion. To fay 'I cannot,' is childifh; and 'I will not,' womanifh."

"I am no herald to inquire of men's pedigrees; it fufficeth me if I know their virtues."

"In nothing had nature done fo much for them, as that it had made them Lords of Truth, whereon all other goods are builded."

A fimilar dignity of mind appears in the conduct of the ftory. One rarely finds, in the fictions of any period, more truly noble and generous characters than thofe of the two princes and two princeffes whofe adventures form the chief part of this romance. Every act and thought of theirs is pervaded by the fame lofty tone. That fhame is worfe than death, that floth is worfe than painful wounds, that felfifhnefs is hateful, friendfhip lovely, courtefy manly, and rudenefs brutifh; fuch is the ftrain of honour implied throughout the Arcadia. The extravagance with which it is carried out goes, it is true, beyond nature and propriety. Neverthelefs, this romantic fpirit is perhaps more faithful to the beft qualities of humanity, than that of any clafs of fiction which has followed until a very recent time. Comparing the Arcadia with the moft celebrated poems in profe and verfe which may be referred to the fame ftandard, it exhibits a fingular delight in portraying virtue. Even Scott is lefs confpicuoufly marked by this characteriftic. To exhibit goodnefs by means of an elaborate contraft with its oppofite is the plan of one great fchool of fiction, of which Clariffa may be named as the type. Another prefers to trace the features of moral excellence in the midft of outward circumftances which are mean and repulfive. A third fchool aims at reprefenting the lights and fhades of human life and character with the impartial truth of a photograph. While each of thefe methods has its own peculiar worth, Sidney's has the air of frefhnefs and hopefulnefs which diftinguifhes youth from age. He may be confidered as happy in living at a time when the crudenefs of art was compenfated by the new afpect which all things wore; when juft fentiments had not yet come by reiteration to pafs for truifms, nor ideal characters to feem imaginary. There are, however, in the Arcadia blemifhes which have been already noticed; and there are faults of compofition which would be intolerable in a modern novel. The ftory, though ingenioufly conftructed, is involved, and bears traces of the curfory manner in which it was written. The incidents from firft to laft are fo improbable, to ufe no ftronger term, that the

reader is perfuaded to follow them with intereft
only by the charm of Sidney's thoughts and language; and the great length at which every particular is related appears exceffive, after making
large allowance for varieties of tafte in this
refpect.

The main fubject of the romance is the court-
fhip of the two difguifed princeffes, Pamela and
Philoclea, by the two princes Mufidorus and
Pyrocles, alfo difguifed. This plot is interwoven
with many epifodes, one of which is the original
of the ftory of Glofter in King Lear. Perhaps
the moft pleafing of all is the epifode of Argalus
and Parthenia, which has been more than once
publifhed feparately, and is ftill fold in a cheap
form by hawkers. Argalus loves Parthenia, and
is loved in return. His difappointed rival finds
an opportunity to rub her face with corrofive
poifon, which deftroys her beauty beyond all hope
of recovery. The love of Argalus for her remains
unaltered, but fhe refufes to difgrace him in the
eyes of the world by becoming his wife, and
fecretly efcapes to Corinth; where fhe is cured
by the queen's phyfician, and reftored to her
former lovelinefs. Returning to Argalus fhe pre-
tends to be a friend of Parthenia, and to bear from
her dying lips a requeft that he fhould accept her-

felf as Parthenia's fubftitute. Argalus, though greatly perplexed, continues faithful to his firft affection, and refufes until, to his joy, Parthenia makes herfelf known to him. They are married, and live together for a time in perfect happinefs. But war breaks out, and Argalus is fent for by the king.

"The meffenger made fpeed, and found Argalus at a caftle of his own, fitting in a parlour with the fair Parthenia; he reading in a book the ftories of Hercules, fhe by him, fo as to hear him read: but while his eyes looked on the book, fhe looked on his eyes, and fometimes ftaying him with fome pretty queftion; not fo much to be refolved of the doubt, as to give him occafion to look upon her; a happy couple, he joying in her, fhe joying in herfelf; but in herfelf, becaufe fhe enjoyed him. Both increafed their riches by giving to each other."

Argalus is wanted to take up the challenge of Amphialus, a chivalrous prince whofe love for one of the king's daughters has provoked the war. They fight, equipped in rich armour, which is minutely defcribed, and after a long and terrible combat Argalus is killed before Parthenia's eyes. Shortly afterwards a ftrange knight arrives in the royal camp.

" He had before him four damſels and ſo many
behind him, all upon palfreys, and all apparelled
in mourning weeds : each of them a ſervant of
each ſide, with like liveries of ſorrow. Himſelf
in an armour, all painted over with ſuch a cunning
of ſhadow that it repreſented a gaping ſepulchre :
the furniture of his horſe was all of cypreſs branches,
wherewith in old time they were wont to dreſs
graves. . . . . The Knight of the Tomb (for ſo
the ſoldiers termed him) ſent to Baſilius to demand
leave to ſend a damſel into the town to call out
Amphialus."

Amphialus accepts the ſtranger's challenge,
and having croſſed over to the little iſland which
ſerved for liſts, " deſired to ſpeak with him ; but
the Knight of the Tomb, with ſilence, and drawing his horſe back, ſhowed no will to hear nor
ſpeak." At the firſt courſe the unknown knight
miſſed his lance-reſt ; and Amphialus gallantly let
his own point paſs over the head of his antagoniſt.
Notwithſtanding this favour, the courteous Amphialus gains an eaſy victory, and ſeeing how far
he is the ſuperior in arms, would have diſmiſſed
his challenger ; but the other provokes him by
inſults into giving an angry blow, which touches
a vital part. He pulls off the helmet which hid
the features of the dying knight ; about whoſe

ſhoulders there fell immediately "the treaſure of fair golden hair which, with the face, witneſſed that it was Parthenia."

The courſe of the romance leads to incidental mention of matters of ſtate and ſociety, the treatment of which is remarkable. As often as occaſion ariſes they are handled as gravely as if actual events were concerned. Queſtions of government, education, law, and even theology, no leſs than building and gardening, are diſcuſſed with a philoſophical ſeriouſneſs which gives to the moſt fantaſtic incidents a certain air of reality. Pamela diſcourſes in priſon upon the firſt principles of religious belief and truſt in Providence, and her prayer has been referred to already.

A ſpecimen, on a ſmaller ſcale, of Sidney's thoughtful manner, is the following deſcription of hawking :—"Upon the ſide of the foreſt they had both greyhounds, ſpaniels and hounds, whereof the firſt might ſeem the lords, the ſecond the gentlemen, the laſt the yeomen of dogs. A caſt of merlins there was beſides, which flying of a gallant height over certain buſhes would beat the birds that roſe down into the buſhes, as falcons will do wild fowl over a river. But the ſport which for that day Baſilius would principally ſhow to Zelmane was the mounting at a Heron; which getting up on his waggling wings with pain, till he was come to fome height (as though the air next the earth were not fit for his great body to fly through), was now grown to diminifh the fight of himfelf and to give example to great perfons, that the higher they be the lefs they fhould fhow. Then a Ger-falcon was caft off after her, who ftraight fpying where the prey was, fixing her eye with defire, and guiding her way by her eye, ufed no more ftrength than induftry. For as a good builder to a high tower will not make his ftair upright, but winding almoft the full compafs about, that the fteepnefs be the more infenfible, fo fhe, feeing the towering of her purfued chafe, went circling and compaffing about, rifing fo with the lefs fenfe of rifing, and yet finding that way fcantly ferve the greedinefs of her hafte, as an ambitious body will go far out of the direct way to win to a point of height which he defires. So would fhe as it were turn tail to the heron, and fly quite out another way, but all was to return to a higher pitch; which once gotten, fhe would either beat with cruel affaults the heron, who was now driven to the beft defence of force, fince flight would not ferve, or elfe clafping with him came down together."

Arcadia not only forms a large part of Sidney's

whole literary works, but reflects his own mind fo vividly, that the examination of its chief characteriftics is effential to a complete view of his life. Its relation to Sidney is often faid to have been ftill more perfonal. He has been fuppofed, though with flight probability, to defcribe himfelf and Fulke Greville in his princes, and Lady Penelope Devereux in his princefs Philoclea. Traditions of this kind have ufually little authority, and there are marked diverfities in the character of the perfons which might be objected to this one in particular. Mufidorus and Pyrocles, Pamela and Philoclea, are artificially contrafted together, and unlike portraits. Sidney, like any other poet, drew his ideas from what he had obferved and felt, according to his own maxim, " Look in thy heart and write." Here and there it is poffible to trace the origin of his fictions. The disfigurement of Parthenia was fuggefted without doubt by Lady Penelope's fuffering from the fmallpox, and her recovering without lofs of beauty. It may be conjectured that Elizabeth was in his mind when he wrote thus :—" The Queen of Laconia, one that feemed born on the confines of beauty's kingdom ; for all her lineaments were neither perfect poffeffioners thereof, nor abfolute ftrangers thereto ; but fhe was a queen, and therefore beautiful." But it may well be doubted whether any portraiture is intended by Sidney, except that he modeftly introduces himfelf as a melancholy young fhepherd. The name of Phillifides thinly difguifes his own, and by this name fome of his friends deplored their lofs when he died.

The feveral books of Arcadia are concluded with verfified dialogues and paftoral fongs, in one of which the allufion to Languet, previoufly quoted, is made by Phillifides. Thefe eclogues are a prominent feature in the Italian Arcadia, but Sidney's are often wearifome, and the metres uncouth. His aim was to unite the rich fancy of Italy with Englifh fimplicity and vigour, but he was caught, like the author of Euphues, by fome of the affectations which he denounced. He fails more fignally in the paffages which were defigned to relieve the graver parts with comedy. Humour was wanting in fome meafure to complete Sidney's almoft univerfal genius. General harmony of mind and foul feems in its nature unfavourable to the power of humour; which is either the play of a carelefs mind, or elfe the reaction of an earneft mind againft cares too heavy to be borne. The latter is the grim humour of fatirifts, who feek relief from fad contemplation in irony and mockery; the former is the more common humour of

light-hearted men, who find entertainment everywhere. In men of action this faculty is ufually
weak; and one who is both earneft and hopeful
is leaft of all likely to be a humorift. Deformity,
whether natural or moral, difpleafes him too much
to afford him mere amufement; and his buoyant
fpirit throws off the depreffion which ftrains fome
noble hearts until bitter laughter is the only alter-
native from bitter tears. Still the want of humour
muft be regarded as a defect, not only of literary
power, but of character alfo. It is a gift akin to
charity of a homely fort, and has its true ufe in
foftening the repulfivenefs of things from which
a fine mind would otherwife fhrink with too in-
tolerant a prejudice. To this faftidioufnefs of
tafte Sidney appears to have been inclined, though
it was fubdued by his extreme kindlinefs and
fympathy. Yet it is not only in wit, but in
humanity, that Damœtas and Mopfa fuffer by
comparifon with Touchftone and Audrey.

Arcadia is brought to a conclufion with much
eloquence, but the author confeffes himfelf to be
weary of his tafk. According to a ftatement
which Ben Jonfon made, forty years afterwards,
to Drummond, Sidney entertained the idea of
adapting what he had written to the legends of
King Arthur. If this plan had been executed,

his literary fame would have been extended by the popularity of the fubject. But a national poem could hardly have arifen from fo artificial a procefs; and the want of a noble female character, a fatal defect in the romances of the Round Table, might have compelled Sidney to alter the whole fable, as Spenfer has done in the Faery Queen.

During Sidney's refidence at Wilton he probably wrote his little effay entitled the " Defence of Poefy." We learn from him that the name of poet had fallen into contempt in England. This opinion was not without excufe; for at the period when he wrote the national literature was fcanty and feeble, fhowing no clear prefage of its magnificent outburft a few years later. The age which is called Elizabethan was only beginning. Though Elizabeth had been more than twenty years on the throne, the men whofe names have made hers illuftrious were, for the moft part, unknown and untried. Several had not yet attained to manhood in 1580. Burleigh and Walfingham, it is true, were at the height of their reputation; and Leicefter's inglorious fame had reached its zenith. But of the array of great men who have fet a deep mark on the Englifh character for all time, none had appeared as yet. Shakefpeare's age was fixteen, Bacon's nineteen, Hooker's, Spenfer's, and Raleigh's, about twenty-feven, when Sidney, in 1580, acknowledged the dearth of Englifh literature. The Shepherd's Calendar, the Earl of Surrey's Lyrics, and the works of Lord Buckhurft and his affociates, were the only pieces which he could call to mind as commendable fince Chaucer. But he pleaded earneftly againft the general inference which was drawn from the fcarcity of good poets. Still more earneftly did he vindicate poetry againft another objection fuggefted by the rifing fect of the Puritans, that poetry is effentially untrue, immoral, and a wafte of time.

Sidney's "Defence" begins by an appeal to antiquity. He fhows that poetry is the moft ancient of arts, " the firft light-giver to ignorance;" the earlieft teachers, philofophers, and hiftorians being poets. He urges the dignity of the Roman and Greek names for a poet; the one calling him *vates,* or Prophet, and the other ποιητής, or Maker. He alfo appeals to Scripture, adducing inftances of Divine poetry; in which he includes not only the Pfalms of David, but the Parables of our Lord. For poetry, he contends, is "a fpeaking picture with this end, to teach and delight;" and therefore not reftricted to the form of verfe. "It is not rhyming and verfing that maketh a poet, (no more than a long gown maketh an advocate, who though he fhould plead in armour fhould be an advocate, and no foldier,) but it is that feigning notable images of virtues, vices, and what elfe; with that delightful teaching which muft be the right defcribing note to mark a poet by."

Proceeding to compare poetry in the abftract with philofophy and hiftory, he gives to it the preference over both; on the ground that while the two latter teach, by precept and example refpectively, the knowledge of virtue, poetry moves men to the love of virtue, which is both a more difficult and a higher art. Admitting and deploring the abufe of poetry, efpecially by the comic dramatifts of his own day, he fhows the injuftice of condemning what is good for its abufe, and argues that properly the art of poetry is neither vicious, falfe, nor effeminate, but the contrary.

This effay of Sidney's may claim to take rank among the moft admirable in our language. For pure fentiment, found philofophy, and brilliancy and grace of ftyle, it is unfurpaffed to this day. It is read much lefs than it deferves, partly, perhaps, becaufe Englifh poetry has been fufficient fince Sidney's time to defend itfelf without an advocate. Moreover, his critical remarks on the

works of his day have loft their intereft; and he
has incurred no fmall blame for cenfuring plays
which were forerunners of the richeft dramatic
literature in the world. The recklefs changes of
time and place, the difcordant mixture of tragedy
with coarfe buffoonery, and other features of the
old Englifh drama which Sidney holds up to
ridicule, were ufed by Shakefpeare's genius and
fkill as elements of a more exquifite harmony
than was ever contemplated in the claffical rules
of unity. Hence Sidney is in fome difcredit as a
critic; and yet what Shakefpeare did for tragedy
and comedy was truly confiftent with the principles of Sidney's effay, though the manner of
execution was different from any which he was
able to forefee. Like moft admirers of Greek
and Roman literature, he was led for a time into
the miftake of imitating the ancient metres; and
he has been feverely cenfured for trying to diffuade
Spenfer from the ufe of rhyme.* It is doubtful
whether there was ever fufficient ground for this
charge againft Sidney. In the " Defence of
Poefy" he balances the merits of ancient and
modern metre, and concludes:—"The latter likewife with his rhyme ftriketh a certain mufic to the

---

* Tytler's Life of Raleigh.

ear; and in fine, since it doth delight, though by another way, it obtaineth the same purpose; there being in either sweetness, and wanting in neither majesty." On the other hand, Sidney's influence in the essential part of poetry was of the best kind. Its amount was immense, and extends through that time to the present. He was the first English critic, and the first writer of modern English prose. He was the nation's idol when the greatest Englishmen were about the age which is most subject to enthusiasm. Spenser probably planned the " Faery Queen" in his company: Shakespeare probably in youth read the " Defence of Poesy," and learned there to appreciate the worth of his own art. Thus, while a long train of poets, from Shakespeare and Spenser to Tennyson, have not disdained to imitate Sidney's fancies, the indirect influence of his pure and heroic mind has probably been deeper still.

Sidney's personal connection with the dramatists is curious. While he was at Wilton, in 1580, his sister became mother of William Herbert, afterwards Earl of Pembroke, " the most universally loved and esteemed of any man "* in the next generation, the friend of Shakespeare, and, in all

---

* Clarendon.

probability, the "W. H." to whom Shakefpeare's Sonnets were dedicated.   Ben Jonfon has coupled Lord Herbert's name with Sidney's in the line of his well-known epitaph on the Countefs, "Sidney's fifter, Pembroke's mother."   At the fame Wilton Houfe Philip Maffinger was born in 1584, and received from Sidney his Chriftian name.

Another work which may be referred to this part of his life is a verfion of the Pfalms.   He began this in conjunction with his accomplifhed fifter, and translated the firft forty-two himfelf.* The remainder were finifhed by her.   Sidney's Pfalms want the modern fmoothnefs of verfifica-tion which has become an almoft univerfal art; but they are fuperior to the authorized verfions, old and new, both in religious and poetical feel-ing.   The metres are varied with the fubjects, and the true character of the Pfalms as fpiritual fongs is forcibly conveyed.   For a fpecimen the opening of the thirty-feventh Pfalm may be quoted :—

> " Fret not thyfelf, if thou do fee
>   That wicked men do feem to flourifh,
>   Nor envy in thy bofom nourifh
>   Though ill deeds well fucceeding be.

---

* Singer's Edition : Preface.

" They foon fhall be cut down like grafs,
　And wither like green herb or flower;
　Do well and truft in heavenly power:
　Thou fhalt have both good foot and place."

From his graver ftudies he refrefhed himfelf by
the amufement of planning houfes and gardens.
The Earl of Pembroke's houfe of Houghton near
Ampthill, now in ruins, was built from his defigns.
His tafte in thefe matters inclined to fimplicity,
as appears from his defcription of the houfe of
Kalander, an Arcadian nobleman, which was
" built of fair and ftrong ftones, ... the
lights, doors, and ftairs, rather directed to the ufe
of the gueft than to the eye of the artificer, and
yet as the one chiefly needed, fo the other not
neglected. . . . . . The fervants not fo many
in number as cleanly in apparel and ferviceable in
behaviour. The back fide of the houfe neither
field, garden, nor orchard; or rather it was both
field, garden, and orchard; for as foon as the defcending of the ftairs had delivered them down,
they came into a place cunningly fet with trees of
the moft tafte-pleafing fruits: but fcarcely they
had taken that into their confideration, but they
were fuddenly ftept into a delicate green; of each
fide of the green a thicket, and behind the thickets
again new beds of flowers, which being under the

trees, the trees were to them a pavilion, and they to the trees a mofaic floor."

Probably the months which he fpent at Wilton or at the Earl's neighbouring manor of Clarendon, were the happieft of Sidney's life. His love for his fifter was mutual, and very deep and tender. In fubfequent years he often returned to the purfuits which have been defcribed in this chapter, and forgot in them the difappointments, of which he had many in the world. Yet his nature was fo evenly balanced between contemplation and action that he could not bear to be long fecluded from either. At Wilton he faw the armour of feveral gallant French knights, Montmorenci, Louis of Bourbon, Montpenfier, and others, the fpoils of the brilliant victory of St. Quentin, where the Earl's father had led the Englifh contingent. Sidney looked with impatience on the trophies of martial valour, and longed to carry out into practice the ideal of Chriftian chivalry which his imagination had conceived.

CHAPTER V.

RETURN TO PUBLIC LIFE.

" Life is a bufinefs, not good cheer."
GEORGE HERBERT.

IN January, 1581,* Sidney was returned to Parliament as Knight of the Shire for Kent. The moft important proceedings of this Parliament, which only fat for a few weeks, were a petition to the Queen to take care for the maintenance of " Mariners and of Navigation, the very ftrength and walls of her Majefty's realm;" and Sir W. Mildmay's Committee for drawing up " fuch laws as would fecure the kingdom againft the Pope and his ad-

---

* This date is 1580 in the Commons' Reports; according to the old way of reckoning, the end of the year. But it is ftyled the 23rd of Elizabeth.

herents." Of that celebrated committee Sidney
was a member. The nation was violently excited
againſt the Roman Catholics, partly from apprehenſion of miſchief from the Queen's impending
marriage with Anjou; partly from diſcoveries
which had been recently made of prieſts intriguing
as ſecret agents of ſedition. The College of Douai
had been founded by Philip of Spain for the purpoſe of training up Engliſh youths in the old religion, and under his own political influence. A
ſimilar college had been inſtituted at Rheims by
the Cardinal of Lorraine, uncle of the Duke of
Guiſe and of Mary, Queen of Scots. From theſe
ſeminaries and from Rome the pupils returned to
England devoted ſervants of the Pope, with hearts
and minds ſkilfully weaned from patriotic affection by the ſophiſtry of the Jeſuits. Loyola's
Society had already begun to recover, by zeal and
diſcipline, the failing hold of the Papacy on
Chriſtendom. The devotion of the Jeſuits as
miſſionaries in India, Japan, and America, their
learning among ſcholars, and their craft among
politicians, extended the power of the Church of
Rome on every ſide. The more pious among
them gained reſpect by their auſtere and ſelf-
denying lives. The more artful undermined the
principles of the Reformation by imbuing the

fchools with a falfe and pernicious fyftem of morals. Confciences were led, under their direction, away from the love of truth in belief and in practice. For truth they fubftituted Papal authority, on the ftrength of which their hearers were taught to be-lieve the moft palpable impoftures, and to commit the darkeft treafon without compunction. Cafes were noted in their books under which lying, falfe fwearing, and affaffination became lawful; and the fupreme teft of lawfulnefs was the fanction of the Pope. Againft Elizabeth no attempt was criminal; for Pius V. had denounced her as a heretic, fchifmatic, and ufurper, and had abfolved her fubjects from their allegiance. Jefuits pro-mulgated againft her and her counfellors the fouleft libels, and their followers were continually plotting the overthrow of her government, not feldom aiming at her life. It was therefore thought neceffary by Parliament to ufe very ftringent meafures for the Queen's protection. Her life was juftly regarded as effential to the welfare of the kingdom. Sidney compared her* to the brand in the legend of Meleager:—"Whenever fhe perifhes, farewell to all our quietnefs."

From Sidney's childhood he had been brought

---

* Letter to Count of Naffau: Pears.

up in a ftrong perfuafion of the falfehood and danger of Romifh doctrines; and this had been confirmed by his foreign experience and by his intercourfe with Languet. The refult of the fittings of Sir W. Mildmay's Committee appeared in laws the feverity of which cannot be juftified. Whoever became reconciled to Rome, or aided in reconciling another, was declared to be guilty of treafon. Any one who faid mafs was liable to a year's imprifonment, and a fine of 100 marks. Abfence from church for a month was punifhable by a fine of 20*l.* But the Papal agents are chiefly to blame for the hardfhips which were fuffered in confequence of thefe laws by peaceful and loyal Catholics; for their doctrines had fhaken in their friends the very foundations of good faith and juftice, and provoked their foes to retaliate. One of thefe agents, Campian, a man of great zeal and talents, who had been at Oxford and afterwards at Douai, was arrefted; and his confeffion, extorted on the rack, tended, whether true or falfe, to exafperate the people ftill more. He was hanged at Tyburn while the Duke of Anjou was in England, profecuting in perfon his fuit for Elizabeth's hand.

The French King fent, in April, a fplendid embaffy, to draw up the articles of marriage in

preparation for the arrival of Anjou himfelf. The ambaffadors were very gracioufly received by the Queen, and magnificently entertained. On Whit-Monday the noblemen of her Court prepared for them a ftately pageant, which was called a "Triumph." Here we meet again with Sidney at the Court. From Languet's correfpondence it feems likely that William of Orange may have reconciled Anjou to him; and the Court is faid to have been "maimed without his company." The "triumph," which is defcribed at vaft length in Stow's Chronicle, gives a lively picture of this fort of diverfions, in which Elizabeth delighted, and of which Sidney was a great inventor. At one end of the tilt-yard at Whitehall was a gallery, which was named for the occafion the Caftle of Perfect Beauty, and here the Queen herfelf fat. Four knights, calling themfelves the Fofter-children of Defire, delivered to her by a page an allegorical meffage, announcing their intention to lay fiege to the caftle, and giving a general challenge to any knights to venture with lance and fword in its defence. Thefe four challengers were the Earl of Arundel, Lord Windfor, Mr. Philip Sidney, and Mr. Fulke Greville. Sidney's appearance with his retinue is thus minutely defcribed :—
"Then proceeded Mafter Philip Sidney in very

fumptuous manner, with armour part blue and the reft gilt and engraven, with four fpare horfes, having caparifons and furniture very rich and coftly, as fome of cloth of gold embroidered with pearl, and fome embroidered with gold and filver feathers, very richly and cunningly wrought." He had four pages that rode on his four fpare horfes, followed by thirty gentlemen and yeomen, and four trumpeters, all gaily attired in yellow and filver; " and they had upon their coats a fcroll or band of filver that came fcarf-wife over the fhoulder, and fo down under the arm, with this pofy or fentence written both before and behind, *Sic nos non nobis.*" The allufion feems to be to Anjou, as being the real winner of the prize to which Sidney and his fellow-challengers made their mimic fiege. Sidney was noted for the variety and fancy of his mottoes. Several occur in the Arcadia. One of his own, *Sine refluxu,* correfponds with Hampden's famous device, *Veftigia nulla retrorfum.* Another expreffes a fimilar refolution not to yield to adverfe circumftances: *Aut viam inveniam, aut faciam;* while another obfcurely implies, what he elfewhere uttered plainly, that he would not' owe his worth to family or fortune: *Vix ea noftra voco.*

The tournament was held for two days, and

was interfperfed with complimentary fpeeches to the Queen. Among other mafques two knights, perfonating Adam and Eve, with long hair over their armour, prefented addreffes to her; and cannon loaded with fweet-fcented powder were fired off from a canvas fort, with many more fuch contrivances. After holding their ground againft all comers with fuccefs, the challengers fent to the Queen a page in afh-coloured garments, bearing an olive-branch in his hand. They afked pardon of her Majefty; they acknowledged their rafhnefs and prefumption in attempting the caftle where Perfect Beauty together with Virtue was enthroned in her perfon; and they made to her their humble fubmiffion.

On this occafion Sidney had the happinefs of being diftinguifhed above all others, as appears from the following, the beft known of his fonnets:—

" Having this day my horfe, my hand, my lance,
    Guided fo well that I obtained the prize,
    Both by the judgment of the Englifh eyes,
And of fome fent from that fweet enemy France,
Horfemen my fkill in horfemanfhip advance:
    Town folks my ftrength: a daintier judge applies
    His praife to fleight which with good ufe doth rife:
Some lucky wits impute it but to chance:
    Others, becaufe of both fides I do take
My blood from them who did excel in this,

> Think Nature me a man of arms did make.
>   How far they ſhot awry! The true cauſe is,
> Stella looked on, and from her heavenly face
> Sent forth the beams which made ſo fair my race." *

The concluding lines refer to Lady Penelope Devereux, for whom his love had increaſed rather than abated with time. But a bitter diſappointment was in ſtore for him. She was forced, not long after this tournament, into a marriage with a man whom ſhe hated. Robert Lord Rich, having ſucceeded in this year to his title and large eſtates, was accepted by the Counteſs as her daughter's huſband. He was a rough and illiterate man, and of a mean diſpoſition. His wealth and influence, however, were ſuch that he was raiſed by James I. to the earldom of Warwick. When this unfortunate marriage took place, Sidney was broken-hearted. He could not refrain from giving utterance to his grief, and to his indignant ſcorn of his churliſh rival. Overmaſtered by his thoughts, as he himſelf ſays of his poetry, he expreſſed them in a number of ſonnets. Theſe, with others previouſly written, were collected and printed after his death under the title of "Aſtrophel and Stella." Sidney is Aſtrophel, and Lady Rich is Stella. For

---

* Sonnet XLI.

beauty of thought and expreſſion theſe poems are juſtly celebrated; but they caſt a blot upon the purity of Sidney's name.

In ſaying ſo much, however, it is neceſſary to defend his memory from aſperſions which have been founded on a ſuperficial reading of the Sonnets. He was not, as he has been ſometimes repreſented, a man of lax morals. The whole of his blameleſs life is a vindication of his character againſt any doubtful inference from his own verſes; and theſe prove nothing more clearly than his keen moral ſenſibility. No ſimilar writings in any time exhibit more finely the ſtruggle in a noble mind between conſcience and paſſion, with the final victory of the right; and, according to the taſte of the period, they muſt be judged to be pure in expreſſion alſo. Sidney's fame has been his chief enemy. Words which were never meant for other eyes, but poured out of his overburdened heart in ſecret or in ſtrict confidence, have been publiſhed to the world. Thus his fancies, wiſhes, and regrets, long ſince repented of with tears, are exhibited as deliberate and ſhameleſs: fact and fiction are indiſcriminately mingled; and in the confuſion of earlier and later ſonnets all are ex-poſed to the blame of a time when his love could no longer be lawful. It is a cruel treachery of

friendſhip when a dead man's private words are
ſubmitted without explanation to the riſk of
wrong. Much depends on the true order of the
pieces in Aſtrophel and Stella. But neither this
nor the date can be precifely determined. It is
likely that the twenty-fourth Sonnet, in which
alluſion is made to Lord Rich, was written after
the thirtieth, which treats of foreign politics, apparently in 1580, and the forty-firſt, of which his
ſucceſs in the tournament is the ſubject. The
fourth ſong, which follows the eighty-fifth Sonnet,
was evidently written while Philip and Penelope
were inmates of Leiceſter Houſe together. More
indications of irregular arrangement in the order
of the Sonnets may be obſerved by careful ſtudy.

We have Sidney's own teſtimony to the reſerve
and delicacy of his love, in a form which makes
it indiſputable :—

> " Becauſe I breathe not love to every one,
>   Nor do not uſe ſet colours for to wear,
>   Nor nouriſh ſpecial locks of vowed hair,
> Nor give each ſpeech a full point of a groan ;
> The courtly nymphs, acquainted with the moan
>   Of them who in their lips Love's ſtandard bear,
>   ' What he ?' ſay they of me, ' now dare I ſwear
> He cannot love ; no, no, let him alone.'
>   And think ſo ſtill, ſo Stella know my mind :
> Profeſs, indeed, I do not, Cupid's art ;

But you, fair maids, at length this true fhall find,
    That his right badge is but worn in the heart;
Dumb fwans, not chattering pies, do lovers prove;
    They love indeed, who quake to fay they love." *

Simple juftice requires that what in any one's conduct is obfcure fhould be conftrued agreeably to the part which is clear. It is no true candour, but a fpirit of detraction, which would interpret in the worft fenfe queftionable paffages of a good man's life. How much caufe there is to difbelieve that Sidney profeffed without fhame his love for Lady Rich appears further by comparifon of Spenfer's " Aftrophel." In that beautiful elegy, written after Sidney's death, and infcribed to his widow, the name of Stella is given to her, which would be inconceivable if the world had already learned to affociate it with another woman. The author of the " Mourning Mufe of Theftylis" defcribes Lady Sidney more evidently under the name of Stella. A reafonable account of Sidney's Sonnets is that he took his emotions as the ground of poetical fancies, which were fcattered about, as the verfes of poets are apt to be, fome circulating freely, others referved to his moft intimate friends; fo that the perfonal application of

---

* Sonnet LIV.

them was unknown till they were brought together. Thus, for the want of a few lines which might ferve for a key, it is ftill difputed whether Shakefpeare's Sonnets are addreffed to a real or an imaginary friend, and whether to one or more than one.

Whatever blame Sidney's paffion may deferve is mitigated by the ftrongeft claim for excufe. He had been encouraged to regard Penelope Devereux as his affianced wife. His love, originally founded on efteem, had grown with years and familiar acquaintance, and had guarded him from the allurements to which his matchlefs perfonal graces expofed him. He himfelf fays of its effects,—

> " If that be fin which doth the manners frame,
>   Well ftaid with truth in word, and faith of deed,
> Ready of wit, and fearing nought but fhame ;
>   If that be fin which in fixed hearts doth breed
> A loathing of all loofe unchaftity,
> Then love is fin, and let me finful be." *

On the part of Lady Penelope there feems to have been a warm and fincere affection :—

> " When I was forced from Stella, ever dear,—
>   Stella ! food of my thoughts, heart of my heart,—
> Stella ! whofe eyes make all my tempefts clear,
>   By iron laws of duty to depart,

---

* Sonnet XIV.

> Alas! I found that fhe, with me, did fmart:
> I faw that tears did in her eyes appear,
> I faw that fighs her fweeteft lips did part."*

She, however, refolved to do her duty, and urged him to fhake off his finful loveficknefs, declaring,—

> " That love fhe did, but loved a love not blind,
>   Which would not let me, whom fhe loved, decline
> From nobler courfe, fit for my birth and mind;
>   And therefore, by her love's authority,
> Will'd me thefe tempefts of vain love to fly,
>   And anchor faft myfelf on virtue's fhore."†

It would have been well if fhe had in later years been able to practife the virtue which fhe had taught Sidney. Her fubfequent career was guilty and miferable. Her beloved brother Robert, Earl of Effex, was taken from her in his prime, impelled to his ruin by her ambition or pique. She incurred fome rifk of fharing his fate by her defperate efforts to fave him. The hufband to whom fhe had been fold was an object of unceafing averfion to her; and fhe left him for Charles, Lord Mountjoy, afterwards Earl of Devonfhire. In the next reign her marriage to the Earl, while Lord Rich was ftill living, led to her banifhment from the Court. She died foon afterwards.

---

* Sonnet LXXXVII. † Sonnet LXII.

K

The conflict of love and duty agitated Sidney much. At length duty prevailed, and he overcame his paffion in the right way, rifing above it, not wearing it out.* His mind emerged from this great trial without degradation. Even while he was under the influence of the idolatrous and rebellious fpirit from which human love is rarely free, his thoughts partook moft of its nobleft effects, as his own fhepherd defcribes them :—" Hath not the only love of her made us raife up our thoughts above the level of the world? Hath not the defire to feem worthy in her eyes made us, when others were fleeping, to fit viewing the courfe of the heavens? when others were running at bafe, to run over learned writings? when others were marking their fheep, we to mark ourfelves?"

---

* In Mr. Craik's interefting work, " The Romance of the Peerage," " Aftrophel and Stella " is placed feveral years too late. (1. 90.) Sonnet **XXX.** was probably written in 1580 (fee Pears, p. 172); certainly not in 1585, when Maurice, Prince of Orange, was a boy. Mr. Craik's other argument for his date is a curious error. " Sir Phip," in Sonnet LXXXIII, is not " Sir Philip Sidney," but a pet dog or bird. Both Mr. Craik and Mr. Bourne in his recent Memoir (p. 108) take for granted that Lady Rich is the Stella of Spenfer and Bryfkett. But that Stella is manifeftly Sidney's widow, who was with him when he died. The ufe of Stella's name is an evidence that Sidney's firft love had long paffed from fact into poetry.

In the end his foul, faddened yet chaftened, rofe like Spenfer's from earthly to heavenly love, as he expreffes in a fonnet which fhould have been printed with the reft, with its concluding motto, " *Splendidis longum valedico nugis.*"

" Leave me, O love ! which reaches but to duft,
   And thou, my mind, afpire to higher things,
Grow rich in that which never taketh ruft,
   Whatever fades, but fading pleafure brings ;
Draw in thy beams, and humble all thy might
   To that fweet yoke, where lafting freedoms be,
Which breaks the clouds, and opens forth the light
   That doth both fhine, and give us eyes to fee.
O take faft hold !   Let that light be thy guide,
   In this fmall courfe which birth draws out to death ;
And think how ill becometh him to flide,
   Who feeketh heav'n, and comes of heavenly breath.
Then farewell, world, thy uttermoft I fee.
   Eternal love, maintain thy life in me !"

The fame year, 1581, brought Sidney another forrow in the death of Languet. Their friend-fhip continued to the laft unabated. Shortly before his death, Languet wrote expreffing a tender concern for Sidney's health, and urging him to marry. He feems to have heard of his unhappy attachment, but not to have known the circumftances. The wife of Du Pleffis Mornay attended upon him in his laft illnefs ; and he was buried at Antwerp, where he died, with much honour, being followed to the grave by the Prince of Orange. Mornay, in the preface to his work on the "Truth of the Chriftian Religion," fpoke with hearty affection of Languet's talents, his modefty, and his exemplary life and death.

Sidney would now have welcomed any offer of active employment; and a propofal was made to him which he would have accepted if the Queen's permiffion could have been obtained. The popular claimant to the throne of Portugal, Don Antonio, folicited him in a flattering letter to join his expedition. Antonio's title to the throne was not good, but the kingdom had been violently feized by Philip of Spain in the abfence of any direct heir; and the Portuguefe preferred an illegitimate prince to a foreigner. There was no nearer reprefentative of Don Sebaftian, who had perifhed with his army in Morocco in 1578, the laft of the Crufaders. He was alfo fupported, though not openly, by England and France. Several Englifh gentlemen volunteered to affift him in making war againft the King of Spain; but he wrote to Sidney that "although many more fhould come, if you are abfent I fhall fay I have not my proper number." To Sidney the expedition was doubly attractive. He defired to ferve in a campaign,

and he defired to ferve againſt Philip; for he was
impatient to fee the time when England ſhould
face the conteſt which he knew to be impending,
and throw down the gauntlet to the Spaniard.
He often converfed with Fulke Greville on the
neceffity of aiding the revolted Netherlands, and
of fitting out a navy to attack the poffeffions of
Spain in the Indies. Under the religious pro-
feffions of Philip and of the Inquifition, he faw
a deep fcheme for uprooting all feeds of freedom
utterly. He was incredulous as to the reality of
the fuperftition which certainly was one of the
ruling motives of the grim and fullen tyrant.
He recognized in Philip's zeal only an engine of
his felfifh policy; and warming with indignation,
he would fay, " that tyrants were no anointed
deputies of God, but of the prince of darknefs."
Such had been Languet's doctrine, and the fubject of a treatife which he left unfiniſhed at his
death. The fame theory was promulgated on
the oppofite fide by the houfe of Guife, and with
fatal effects; for its refults were the affaffination
of two fucceffive kings of France, Henry III. and
Henry IV. In the following century a fimilar
doctrine, found among the papers of Algernon
Sidney, was the chief evidence that led to his
unjuſt conviction. It is one of the many partial

truths which none but the moſt juſt and loyal minds can bear to entertain without drawing from them fallacious and deadly conſequences.

The proſpect of ſucceſs with Don Antonio ſeems to have been very faint and viſionary. He wanted apparently that force of character which is indiſpenſable in the leader of a war of independence. But Sidney was prevented from joining him by Elizabeth's refuſal to give him leave of abſence. She was ſtill reluctant to compromiſe herſelf with the king of Spain, and ſhe was alſo apt to be unwilling to ſpare her lords and gentlemen from the kingdom. With ſomething of a mother's impatience of ſeparation from her children, the great Queen conſented with difficulty to foreign expeditions, and recalled them on ſlight pretexts. She found for Sidney ſome employment on confidential ſervice at home, the nature of which cannot be aſcertained more preciſely : In the Burleigh Papers there is a letter from Sidney to the Queen dated Graveſend, Nov. 10, 1581. He writes :—

" This rude piece of paper ſhall preſume, becauſe of your Majeſty's commandment, moſt humbly to preſent ſuch a cipher as little leiſure could afford me. If there come any matters to

my knowledge the importance of which fhall deferve to be fo marked, I will not fail (fince your
pleafure is my only boldnefs) to your own hand
to recommend it. In the mean time I befeech
your Majefty will vouchfafe legibly to read my
heart in the courfe of my life, and though itfelf be
but of a mean worth, yet to efteem it like a poor
houfe well fet. I moft humbly kifs your hands, and
pray God your enemies may then only have peace
when they are weary of knowing your force."

Sidney's correfpondence with the Queen may
be conjectured to have fome reference to French
politics, in which he was afterwards employed by
her, notwithftanding the ftrong language he had
ufed of the Houfe of Valois and of the negotiation
with the Duke of Anjou. In the fame month of
November Anjou arrived in England, and the
nuptials feemed to be imminent. For nearly
three months the nation was in fufpenfe, while the
Queen vacillated between prudence and inclination. At length, in February, he made up his
mind that he was only wafting time, and departed
for his government in the Netherlands. Elizabeth parted from him reluctantly, and accompanied him as far as Canterbury. She alfo fent a
fplendid train of noblemen and gentlemen as his

efcort; Leicefter, Lord Howard, the Vice-Admiral, Lord Hunfdon, Lord Willoughby, Lord Sheffield, Sidney, Raleigh, and 500 more. They were delayed by unfavourable weather; but on the 17th, having arrived in the Scheld, Anjou was received by the firft nobles and citizens of the United Provinces. He took the cuftomary oaths as Duke of Brabant, outfide the gates of Antwerp, in the prefence of the Prince of Orange and his youthful fon Maurice. A fucceffion of feafts and pageants followed with magnificent proceffions, for which Belgium has long been celebrated. Allegorical figures perfonating Religion, Juftice, Prudence and Fortitude, Patriotifm and Patience, greeted the Duke, who was foon, however, to difpel the fair hopes which afcribed thefe virtues to him. In violation of hofpitality, gratitude, and oaths the moft folemn and reiterated, he confpired to feize and fack Antwerp, and to make his fovereignty abfolute. The courage of the citizens defeated his attempt, but the bafenefs which he fhowed confirmed the worft auguries of Sidney.

For fome time after this fhort vifit to the Netherlands, Sidney appears to have been unemployed in any public capacity. He fought in vain for a career in which he might do honourable fervice to his country. He applied to the

Lord Treasurer to be joined with the Earl of Warwick in the administration of the Ordnance Office. "I desire it more," he said, "for the being busied in a matter of some serviceable experience, than for any other commodity, which I think is but small that can be made of it." The Earl desired that this arrangement should be made for his nephew, and the Queen gave her consent. But impediments were thrown in the way, and Sidney wrote the following characteristic letter to Burleigh :—

"Right Honourable my Singular
      Good Lord,

"Without carrying with me any further reason of this boldness than your well-known goodness unto me, I humbly crave of your Lordship your good word unto her Majesty for the confirming of the grant she once made unto me of joining me patent with the Earl of Warwick, whose desire is that it should be so. The larger discovering whereof I will omit as superfluous to your wisdom, neither will I use more plenty of words, till God make me able to print them in some serviceable effect towards your Lordship. In the mean time I will pray for your long and prosperous life, and so humbly take my leave.

" At Ramſbury, this 20th of July, 1583. Your Lordſhip's moſt humbly at commandment,

" PHILIP SIDNEY."

He ſtill maintained private, though not intimate, friendſhip with Burleigh; for about the ſame time he wrote to him, touching gracefully the loſs which the Treaſurer had ſuſtained by the death of his daughter's huſband, Mr. Wm. Wentworth:—

" I came up hoping to have been myſelf a deliverer of the encloſed letter, and ſo to have laid my father's mind and matters in your Lordſhip's hand, as on whoſe advice and diſcretion he dependeth. But finding here the loſs that your Lordſhip hath of late had, it made me both at firſt delay the ſending and now the bringing; leſt, becauſe we were dear friends and companions together, my ſight might ſtir ſome grief in your Lordſhip."

Sidney obtained at length the appointment to the Ordnance Office, but not without two years' more delay. His patent is dated July 21, 1585. This part of his life illuſtrates the truth of the familiar lines,—

> " There is a tide in the affairs of men
> Which, taken at the flood, leads on to fortune
> Omitted, the remainder of the voyage
> Is bound in ſhallows."

Such a tide had offered itfelf to him. Birth, genius, royal favour, ariftocratic connection, efficient fervice rendered to the State, concurred to raife him at the age of twenty-three to the top of the wave of honour. Yet after the lapfe of fix years he was advanced no further. His father had propofed that he fhould be affociated with himfelf in the government of Ireland, when it was thought likely to be offered to him once more; but the plan had fallen to the ground. He was ftill Mr. Philip Sidney. Men whofe qualities were in all refpects poor compared with his, had furpaffed him in the race for worldly pofition. His great influence with the Queen and her chief advifers had been ufed and partially confumed during thefe years without any material advantage to himfelf. It had been fpent in recommending others to favour; obfcure men of genius, poor poets, poor muficians, poor foldiers, and men of all kinds who either deferved or needed patronage; and he had rifked his whole intereft for his country's good, when he endeavoured to diffuade the Queen from a marriage on which her heart was fet. She feems never to have liked him from that time forward. " She was very apt," Walfingham faid, " on every light occafion to find fault with him." Yet it muft be allowed that fhe had fome excufe, and her conduct to Sidney was in the main generous and royal. She admired his character, and recognized his merits with a good grace, though often tardily. But the Lord Treafurer ftood in his way. The intrepid franknefs, which captivated while it provoked Elizabeth, had no charms for Burleigh. He was both diftruftful and jealous of him, as mere politicians are apt to be of a truly magnanimous man. Sharing the French diplomatift's horror of zeal, he fhrank, perhaps without any ill will towards Sidney, from ufing his fervices; and it was a part of his policy, as Bacon obferved and felt, to keep able men in the background. Sidney was accufed to the Queen of ambition, becaufe he bore his forced inaction impatiently; and of pride, becaufe he difdained the mean arts of courtiers. But if he failed to float forward on the tide which would have borne him to fortune, it was mainly the refult of his own choice. He had fet his fails another way, adopting the counfel of his favourite lines from Horace :—

> " You better fure fhall live not evermore
> Trying high feas."

The aim of his life had been neither fortune nor glory, but to live well. He had his reward in the praife and love of the worthieft men of his own and of all fucceeding times, and a ftill higher witnefs in his confcience that he had chofen the right path. It is hardly a matter for furprife or regret that he miffed the vulgar prizes of a fuc-cefsful life. Thofe who enjoy continued profpe-rity in ftate affairs, have commonly to lay afide fome virtuous fcruples, which cannot be deemed faftidious, for they preferve the whitenefs of the foul.

Some unpublifhed MS. notices among the State Papers occupy, though very imperfectly, a vacant fpace in Sidney's biography which has hitherto appeared a blank. His name occurs from time to time in correfpondence with various perfons, always in a pofition of fome weight and influence, though not fuch as to alter materially the prevail-ing impreffion that his fervices were little ufed. He feems to have been appointed Captain of the Ifle of Wight, in March, 1583. His name occurs with the rank of General of Horfe, in a mufter roll of the army, in 1584; and he is fent with fome authority to Dover to confult with the Royal commiffioners upon the repair of the harbour. He is alfo implicated in numerous private matters, fometimes fuing for favours for his friends, making up quarrels, or interceding with the Spaniards for an Englifh failor condemned to die for piracy.

At another time he appears in the lefs pleafing afpect of being enriched, unwillingly, from the fines paid by recufants. Altogether Sidney led a bufy though certainly not an eventful life at that time. But the world prefented fo many grand enterprifes, that what would in another age have been only laudable ftillnefs and contentment, appeared then as no better than floth.

Sidney meditated various fchemes at his leifure, among which he chiefly inclined to American difcovery. His imagination had long ago been excited by the reports of Frobifher and his companions, one of whom brought from Nova Scotia a nugget of gold which raifed high expectations in England, though it proved in the end to be worth no more than as much good building ftone. Languet, with his ufual caution and forethought, had warned him againft the fnare of the Indies:— "Beware," he faid, "left the accurfed thirft of gold fhould creep into a mind which has hitherto admitted nothing but the love of truth and an anxiety to deferve well of all men." More recently his intereft in the unexplored marvels of the Weft, had been revived by the publication, in 1582, of Hakluyt's "Divers Voyages touching the Difcovery of America and the Iflands adjacent," which was dedicated to Sidney. "We are half perfuaded," he wrote to Sir Edward Stafford, the ambaſſador at Paris, " to enter into the journey of Sir Humphrey Gilbert very eagerly, whereunto your Mr. Hakluyt hath ſerved for a very good trumpet." Hakluyt in his dedication craves of Sidney pardon for overboldneſs, truſting alſo that he will " continue and increaſe his accuſtomed favour towards theſe godly and honourable diſcoveries." His book is an account of the voyages of Cabot and others, and an attractive deſcription of Florida, originally addreſſed to Francis I. of France, by one Verazzano. Under the name of Florida is compriſed the whole coaſt of the preſent Slave States of America. This country is deſcribed as being fupplied with the richeſt natural wealth: gold, ſilver, copper, lead, turquoiſes and pearls, " in ſo marvellous abundance as is ſcarce credible," ſome of them being as big as acorns. A ſoil of great fertility, bearing two crops of wheat in the year; firs, vines of great ſize, all kinds of plants, and " in ſhort, nothing lacking for the life of man." Fair havens for ſhips at all tides, large rivers, a temperate climate, " marvellous pleaſant," ſo that in the hotteſt time of year the ſailors had no ſickneſs in thirty-eight degrees of latitude. The people " of a good and ſerviceable nature, which will be content to ſerve thoſe that ſhall with gentleneſs and humanity go about to allure them, as it is needful for thofe that be fent thither hereafter fo to do." In addition to the advantages of a fettlement on this coaft, Hakluyt encourages the hope of difcovering the great queft of Atlantic navigators, a north-weft paffage to the Indies. He fubmits reafons for expecting to find a paffage in lat. 58°, where the name of Frobifher's Strait preferves the track of that famous feaman, and the delufive opening of Hudfon's Bay explains the author's error. A map of the fuppofed route is added; and Hakluyt propounds as a phyfical law the hardy axiom, "Nature has made no fea unnavigable, nor land unhabitable."

Sidney had poffibly been ftill further allured towards thefe adventures by the eloquent tongue of Walter Raleigh, Sir Humphrey Gilbert's half-brother, who fafcinated all who approached him by his dazzling pictures of glory, dominion, and wealth to be gained in the Weft. That wonderful man, who feems the complete imperfonation of the genius and valour of Elizabeth's reign, was nearly of the fame age with Sidney, and they had been at Oxford together. In Court politics they were oppofed, particularly in reference to the French marriage; for Raleigh was a friend of Suffex, under whom he had ferved, and who had been Leicefter's chief rival. In 1579, Raleigh bore Oxford's meſſage to Sidney, propoſing an agreement. In 1582, they were aſſociated in the eſcort of Anjou to the Netherlands. They were alſo united by the cloſer bond of common friend-ſhip for Spenſer. Both were of the ſame mind in deſiring to anticipate the hoſtile deſigns of Spain by increaſing the Engliſh navy and attack-ing the Spaniſh colonies. Both were heartily attached to their native country and to the Pro-teſtant religion. In character, though eſſentially unlike, there were many points of ſympathy be-tween them. Both were men of rare imagina-tion and enterpriſe, eager alike for knowledge and for fame. The talents of each were almoſt equally verſatile. Raleigh was perhaps the ſu-perior in graſp of intellect and force of will, though his reputation dates from a riper time of life than Sidney attained. Sidney's character is marked in contraſt by a reſtleſs aſpiration after a more than earthly ideal. He was ſo made that he could not long contemplate the kingdoms of the world and the glory of them without feeling, by and by, a deep ſenſe of their vanity, however much his fancy might for a time be delighted. The extent of the private acquaintance of Ra-leigh and Sidney is doubtful. In ſome lines,

L

which are believed on good authority to be Raleigh's, written after Sidney's death, he fays,—

> " I that, in thy time and living ftate,
> Did only praife thy virtues in my thought ;"

but thefe verfes, while they make the intimate friendfhip of the two queftionable, feem to imply, fome degree of perfonal knowledge.

Sidney purfued his fcheme of colonization fo far as to obtain a grant of three million acres of American land, yet to be difcovered ; and of this he fold portions to other gentlemen who were difpofed to join in his adventure. Among the State Papers is an indenture by which 30,000 acres of Sidney's eftate are conveyed to Sir George Peckham, of Denham, in Kent.* Happily, however, Sidney did not fail with Sir Humphrey Gilbert. That fatal voyage was undertaken with

---

* Domeftic Series, CLXI. 44. Mr. Bourne has ftated the purport of this deed incorrectly. (Memoir, p. 372.) Sidney did not transfer his whole American eftate to Sir George Peckham. I have ventured (p. 143) to refer Sidney's letter to Sir Edward Stafford on Gilbert's voyage to this time, July, 1583. The date which is given in the Sidney Papers (p. 298), and copied by Mr. Bourne (p. 421), is a year later. But Gilbert's journey was over long before July, 1584.

the faireft hopes. The Queen fent Sir Humphrey a jewel reprefenting an anchor guided by a lady, with a meffage to the effect that fhe wifhed as well to his fhip as if fhe were herfelf on board. But misfortune attended the expedition from the firft. Two fhips out of five, Raleigh's being one of them, were compelled to return, difabled by contagious ficknefs among the crew. Another was wrecked, and a fourth, Sir Humphrey's own, the Squirrel, after having laid claim to Newfoundland, went down with all hands in a ftorm. It has often been related in verfe and profe how he was laft heard encouraging his men in words which became a hero and a Chriftian, "Be of good heart, my friends! we are as near to heaven on the ocean as on land." The remaining veffel, the Golden Hind, returned alone, bearing the news of the acquifition and the difafter.

Next year Raleigh, nothing daunted, fitted out another expedition at his own coft, and with far better fuccefs. He planted the royal ftandard on the American coaft to the north of Florida. In honour of the Virgin Queen he called that whole region Virginia, under which illuftrious name his patent of difcovery and right of fettlement were confirmed to him by a Parliamentary committee, of which Sidney was a member.

In the mean time, Sidney's life, though barren of brilliant achievements, was not idle nor unprofitable. Befides literary works, which have been noticed in the laft chapter, he was engaged in a copious foreign correfpondence. Dupleffis Mornay wrote to him frequently, not only as to a private friend, but regarding Sidney as an able and influential ally of his mafter, the King of Navarre. It is a wide field for fpeculation to inquire what might have been the refult if Sidney's policy of recognizing and aiding the Huguenots had been followed with decifion and conftancy. Perhaps at that time the refources of England were unequal to fuch an effort. In July, 1583, Mornay complained that for three months he had not heard from Sidney, and inquired whether he was married, that fo unufual an interval had occurred in their correfpondence. He had gueffed rightly. Sidney was married during this fummer, having chofen for his wife Frances Walfingham, daughter of the far-fighted and wily ftatefman who had been his faft friend ever fince he had fheltered him, in his boyhood, from the maffacre of Paris. He had alfo become Sir Philip Sidney.

From a few fcattered hints Dame Frances Sidney may be defcribed as a beautiful young girl,

of a homely difpofition little in harmony with her
eventful fortunes. Elizabeth, as her manner was,
fpoke of her flightingly; but fhe feems to have
deferved and earned the affectionate efteem of
her hufband. There is no ground for the affump-
tion which has been made that his heart ftill
wandered after Lady Rich; though the ordinary
courfe of human nature would fuggeft that the
romance of love had forfaken him with her.

The marriage contract was arranged by the
parents. Sir Henry Sidney, in the valuable auto-
biographical letter to Walfingham, to which reference has been made more than once,* fays, " I
rejoice in the alliance with all my heart . . . .
I know that it is the virtue which is, or that
you fuppofe is, in my fon, that you made choice
of him for your daughter, refufing happily far
greater and far richer matches." On the other
hand, he declares bluntly, " If I had regarded
any prefent gain, I might have received a great
fum of money for the goodwill of my fon's marriage, much to the relief of my prefent biting
neceffity." Young men in that day deferred to
their elders in a degree which now appears extraordinary. Thus Philip's relation to Leicefter

---

* State Papers, vol. CLIX. Ludlow, March 1, 1582-3.

had led him, in 1582,* to afk leave to abfent himfelf from Court, for his health and for other reafons, with the fimplicity of a child. Sir Henry defcribes his three fons as "one of excellent good promife, the fecond of great good hope, the third not to be defpaired, but very well to be liked." His eftate, however, was greatly embarraffed. "I am now 54 years of age, toothlefs and trembling, being 5000*l.* in debt, and 30,000*l.* worfe than I was at the death of my moft dear lord and mafter, King Edward VI. Commend me," he concludes, "moft heartily to my good lady, coufin, and fifter, your wife, and blefs and bufs our fweet daughter. And if you will vouchfafe, beftow a bleffing on the young knight, Sir Philip." Sidney had been knighted at Windfor, in January. He was deputed to receive the Order of the Garter at the inftallation of his friend Prince Cafimir,† whom Elizabeth had invefted with her own hands four years before. Thus the honour of which he was moft worthy was conferred upon him by a byway. After being for years renowned throughout Europe as

---

* Collins, i. 392. The date of this letter is doubtful in the manufcript, the numbers being imperfectly formed.

† This circumftance is explained by Mr. Bourne, p. 364.

a pattern of chivalry, he obtained the dignity of knighthood as proxy of another.

Soon afterwards, his attention was called to a matter which touched him very nearly, but in which it cannot be expected or wifhed that others fhould participate in his feelings. An anonymous pamphlet appeared, in 1584, called " Leicefter's Commonwealth," the purpofe of which was to vilify and defame the Earl of Leicefter. It is generally underftood to have been the work of an Englifh Jefuit, Robert Parfons, a man of bad character and indefatigable hoftility to Elizabeth's government. Commencing with a plaufible air of impartiality, this book proceeds to load the Earl with the moft loathfome imputations. While the authorfhip was ftill uncertain, Sidney applied himfelf to defend his uncle; and wrote a reply which was found in manufcript at Penfhurft in the middle of the laft century. This " Defence of Leicefter" has been praifed by Horace Walpole, who otherwife difparages Sidney, as being a favourable fpecimen of his powers. It feems, however, to be no more than a rough draft, not finally prepared for publication; nor is it truly a defence at all. Sidney argues with reafon that the libel is a covert attack upon the Queen through her favourite, and he convicts

the author of fome hiftorical blunders, as well as
of multiplying inconfiftent flanders againft Leicefter. But the greater part of his anfwer is
devoted to an elaborate and fpirited expofure of
the falfehood that the Dudleys were bafe-born,
which touched himfelf. " I truly am glad," he
faid, " to have caufe to fet forth the nobility of
that blood whereof I am defcended, which but
upon fo juft caufe without vainglory could not
have been uttered." As for the accufations from
which Leicefter had real need to be defended,
Sidney paffes them by as merely falfe and ma-
licious; reciting them with fcorn, " diffimulation,
hypocrify, adultery, falfehood, treachery, poifon,
rebellion, treafon, cowardice, atheifm, and what
not." The character which hiftory has delivered
of the Earl to our own time cannot fo lightly be
exonerated from this black catalogue. Yet there
is every reafon for fuppofing that Sidney believed
him to be innocent. Even now the charges are
ftrong fufpicions rather than proved crimes.
On the two graveft, the death of Amy Robfart,
and that of Walter, Earl of Effex, Leicefter was
forward in demanding an inquiry, which feems
in each cafe to have been fairly conducted, and
yet failed to bring home any guilt to him. The
very animofity of his Jefuit affailant is in his

favour, as indicating that his power was adverſe to Papal intereſts. But among his own country-men alſo his guilt or innocence was made a party queſtion, and partiſan attacks were of the bittereſt kind. His rivals in the Queen's favour, and the old enemies of his family, did not ſhrink from uſing any calumny which Jeſuit agents might invent. Hence it was natural that his own nephew and adopted heir ſhould diſdain as ſlan-ders the matters which ſeem to us to call for careful ſifting. Moreover, Robert Dudley was one of the moſt perſuaſive of men, and a profound diſſembler. Though perſonally ſumptuous, and a patron of plays and revels, he was a Puritan in religion, and his diſcourſe was ſeaſoned with pro-teſtations of piety and honeſty. Sidney had the generous weakneſs of being ſomewhat blind to faults in his kindred; and upon no ſubject was his judgment leſs ſure than where they were con-cerned. Leiceſter had been to the Sidneys a conſtant and affectionate friend, beyond what the ties of blood between them demanded. His gracioufneſs of manners, and munificence towards men of letters, contraſted agreeably with the Queen's parſimony and the harſh integrity of Burleigh. It was of ſtill more conſequence, that he was the foremoſt advocate in England of hoftility to the King of Spain and the Pope. Where hypocrify acts like virtue, detection is almoft impoffible. At this particular moment Leicefter was ftraining all his intereft, and preparing to rifk his whole private fortune, for the promotion of the alliance between England and the Netherlands. Whatever felfifh ambition may have been in his own mind, his public conduct for the time was that of a patriot.

The revolt of the Netherlands had reached a crifis. In June, 1584, the Duke of Anjou died of a ftrange and painful difeafe, fweating blood like his brother Charles IX. This event would have been comparatively unimportant, if William of Orange had lived to hold the Provinces together by his commanding influence; but he alfo died a month later, affaffinated by a fanatical Papift. It was no longer poffible for the Dutch to carry on the war againft Spain without foreign affiftance. The inflexible refolution to be free, and the wifdom of their devoted leader, had hitherto been a match for the ftrategy and treafure oppofed to them; but now, without a head, the States were likely to fall afunder. They were willing therefore to offer to France or England the fovereignty of a larger and far more flourifhing territory than the prefent kingdom of Holland, in confideration of being protected in their laws and liberty. If neither France nor England would efpoufe their caufe, they could not much longer refufe Philip's overtures of peace; and peace involved the Spanifh Inquifition, Spanifh garrifons, Spanifh magiftrates, the Mafs, the deftruction of their ancient conftitutions, the lofs of the Bible and of religious freedom, with every conceivable circumftance of oppreffion and revenge. To France, as moft favourably fituated for their defence, they made their firft appeal. It was feconded by a propofal from Elizabeth to Henry. On the occafion of Anjou's death Sidney was chofen * to condole with the King and with the Queen-mother Catharine, and to propofe a league between England and France for the purpofe of giving fuccour to the Netherlands. He was charged to exprefs the Queen's affection for Anjou, her private grief at his lofs, and her hope that the friendfhip which had been between the King and herfelf might continue unbroken. He was directed to call the king's attention to the ftate of the Low Countries in a fecond interview.

" In confequence of the lamented death of the Prince of Orange," Elizabeth propofed that Eng-

---

* Cotton MS. Brit. Mus. Galba, E. vi. 241.

land and France fhould take fome meafures in
concert for defence of " the poor afflicted people
of the Low Countries, who without fome prefent
affiftance will not be able to hold out." She was
willing to make either a fecret or an open league
with Henry; but Sidney was not empowered to
treat any further than to receive propofals. The
French king had already fhown fo much change
and coldnefs that Elizabeth was greatly diffatisfied,
and Sidney was ordered to return with fpeed if he
fhould meet with a cool reception. He did not,
however, go to Paris. His miffion was delayed
at firft by the king's abfence in the fouth of France;
and it was finally abandoned, upon the accounts
which Walfingham received of Henry's difpofition.* Henry, overawed by Guife, fhrank from
the profpect of a war with Spain, added to civil
wars in his own kingdom. During many months
he kept the Dutch in fufpenfe, while he negotiated
with Philip with the view of turning their offer to
his own profit. At length he let the envoys go
with a difcourteous refufal. They then appealed
to England, and Elizabeth received them favourably. She gave them audience without delay, and

---

* MS. State Paper Office. Letters of Sir E. Stafford,
July 23,—Auguft 10, 1584.

explained her intentions in a Latin fpeech with great clearnefs and energy. Abfolutely declining for herfelf the fovereignty of the United Provinces, fhe confented to fend an Englifh army to their affiftance. In doing this, fhe told the deputies, fhe knew fhe would offend the King of Spain as much as if fhe did more. "But what care I?" fhe continues. "We muft all die once. I know very well that many princes are my enemies, and are feeking my ruin; and that where malice is joined with force, malice often arrives at its ends. But I am not fo feeble a princefs that I have not the means and the will to defend myfelf againft them all. They are feeking to take my life, but it troubles me not. He who is on high has defended me until this hour, and will keep me ftill, for in Him do I truft." *

Thus England embarked into the conflict with Spain, for which Sidney had long waited anxioufly. As a foldier he defired to take part in the great continental wars in which Raleigh, Norris, and others of his affociates had already gained renown. But he wifhed for war upon the deeper ground which alone can juftify the wifh, looking to war as the fafeguard of truth and liberty. While his

---

* Motley, United Netherlands, 1.

heart went along with the perfecuted citizens of Ghent, Bruffels, and other famous towns reduced or about to be reduced to fervile mifery, he alfo feared for his own dear country fimilar evils; and he regarded timely refiftance to Philip as the beft means of felf-prefervation. How vital to England was the independence of the States, was fpeedily proved in the year of the Armada, when Parma waited in vain for a fleet to tranfport his fierce veterans acrofs the Channel. The relative condition of Holland and Belgium, a century later, gives the means of comparing the mifchief of war with that of fuch a peace as the King of Spain's.

The Earl of Leicefter was appointed to the command of the army; and Sidney hoped to obtain the poft of governor of Flufhing, one of the towns which were to be held in pledge by the Englifh. He was again difappointed. A rumour reached him that the poft was likely to be given to fome other perfon. More ferious rumours fpread that the Queen had changed her mind, and that the expedition would not proceed. She had indeed fhown fome difpofition to waver in her purpofe, and it was only by means of the ftrenuous efforts of Walfingham and Leicefter that the agreement with the States was carried out. Time was loft in details of negotiation till it was

too late to fave Antwerp, which capitulated in
Auguft, after a fiege which is memorable in hiftory
for the extraordinary fkill and valour which was
difplayed on both fides. And now Sidney gave
up his whole mind to the project which he had
long cherifhed, of founding a colony in the Weft
Indies. His plans were concerted with Sir Francis
Drake, who had lately received knighthood for
his important difcoveries, and for his great though
unfcrupulous fervices as a privateer. They were
not well-afforted companions. In colonization, as
in other things, Sidney placed a lofty ftandard before himfelf. It was his aim to avoid the faults
of thofe who had made colonies of brigands and
fugitives. Like Bacon, he felt that "it is a fhame-
ful and unbleffed thing to take the fcum of people
and wicked condemned men, to be the people
with whom you plant."* Sidney had perfuaded
thirty gentlemen of good family and fortune to
fell 100*l.* worth of land each for the expedition :
he had alfo prevailed on the United Provinces to
engage to affift him with a fecond fleet. Lord
Brooke defcribes him as propofing to all claffes of
honeft men inducements according to their difpofition :—fame, conqueft, and adventure over a

---

† Effay, Of Plantations.

boundlefs expanfe of land and fea, for thofe who
defired it; for the miffionary, the profpect of con-
verting the heathen, and reclaiming the " poor
Chriftians" who had been led aftray by Romifh
idolatry; to the ingenious and induftrious, abundance of natural riches for ufeful arts to work
upon; while the word gold was a general allure-
ment to every fort. It was agreed between Sidney
and Drake that they fhould have the joint command of the fleet; but that, fo long as the expedition was fitting out, the nominal commander
fhould be Drake alone. Sidney kept fecret his
purpofe of failing, for fear of being detained
by the Queen. The fame apprehenfion led him
to ufe artifice in leaving the Court. The fleet,
which Drake was provifioning with funds fupplied
by Sidney, lay at Plymouth. As it happened,
news reached the Court of Don Antonio's expected arrival at that port, at the very time when
Sidney received word that Drake's preparations
were complete. He feized the excufe of going to
meet Don Antonio, and left Richmond without
fufpicion. But on his arrival at Plymouth he
found unexpected delays on the part of Drake.
The fhips had been faid to be ready, waiting only
for a favourable wind; now the wind was favourable, yet no orders were given to fail. At night

Greville confided to Sidney, as they lay awake together, that Drake's procraftination appeared to him wilful. He rejected the fufpicion, but ob: ferved for himfelf, and in a few days he was convinced of its truth. By that time the Queen had notice of Sidney's plan ; and meffengers were fent to ftop his departure, or, in cafe of his refufal, to ftop the fleet. The firft meffenger was intercepted, and deprived of his papers by two of Sir Philip's followers in difguife. The next was a peer of the realm, who threatened him with the Queen's fevere difpleafure if he fhould perfift; at the fame time offering to him the governorfhip of Flufhing with the military rank of general of horfe. Sidney fubmitted to the royal mandate, and Drake fet fail without him on September 17th.

Elizabeth was fo well pleafed with Sidney's obedience that, inftead of punifhing him for this attempt, fhe conferred upon him an unufual honour. While he was preparing to depart for the Netherlands his wife bore him a daughter, and the Queen came up to London from Richmond to be prefent at the chriftening as godmother. This was in November. Immediately afterwards, having paid a fhort vifit to Leicefter at Wanftead, Sidney failed for Flufhing, where he and the fupplies of money which he brought were anxioufly expected.

M

CHAPTER VI.

WAR IN THE NETHERLANDS.

" Auch die Tugend
Hat ihre Helden, wie der Ruhm, das Glück."
WALLENSTEIN'S *Tod.*

FLUSHING is built on the southern shore of the swampy island of Walcheren, which has since acquired a melancholy celebrity in the annals of Great Britain. The climate is unhealthy, especially for foreigners; but the town, from its situation, is of the first military and naval importance. With the two outlying forts of Rammekins and Breskins, on either side of the Scheld, it commands the approach to Antwerp from the sea. Its maritime position is convenient for guarding or threatening the whole coast of the Netherlands; and its ample harbour admits the largest vessels to anchor alongside the quays. Sidney's passage, on Thursday, Nov. 18, was so ſtormy that he was unable to enter the harbour, and landed at Rammekins. He was received at Fluſhing by Edward Norris, a young man of diſtinguiſhed valour, who had landed with the firſt diviſion of the Engliſh contingent, and held the town till the arrival of the governor, who took the oaths of office on Sunday the 21ſt. In the following urgent letter to the Earl of Lei-ceſter, Sidney gives his firſt impreſſions of the ſtate of affairs in Zealand.*

" RIGHT HONOURABLE MY SINGULAR GOOD
     LORD,
" UPON Thurſday we came into this town, driven to land at Ramekins, becauſe the wind began to riſe in ſuch ſort as our maſters durſt not anchor before the town ; and from thence came with as dirty a walk as ever poor governor entered his charge withal. I find the people very glad of me, and promiſe myſelf as much ſurety in keeping this town as popular goodwill, gotten by light hopes and by as ſlight conceits, may breed me ; for indeed the garriſon is far too weak to command by authority, which is pity ; for how great a jewel this is to the crown of Eng-

---

* This and the following letters are copied, with a few un-important emendations, from Mr. Gray's Collection.

land, I need not write to your Lordſhip, who knows it ſo well. Yet, I muſt needs ſay, the better I know it, the more I find the preciouſneſs of it. I have ſent to Mr. Norris for my couſin's Scots company, for Colonel Morgan's, and my brother's (which I mean to put in the Ramekins), but I doubt I ſhall but change, and not increaſe; the enſigns, by any more than mine own company, for fear of breeding jealouſies in this people, which is carried more by ſhows than ſubſtance; and therefore the way muſt be rather to increaſe the number of men in each company, than the companies, and that may be done eaſily enough, with their good liking; but I mean to innovate as little as may be till your Lordſhip's coming, which is here longed for as Meſſias is of the Jews; but indeed moſt neceſſary is it that your Lordſhip make great ſpeed to reform both the Dutch and Engliſh abuſes.

" I am more and more perſuaded that, with that proportion which her Majeſty alloweth, the country is fully able to maintain the wars, if what they do be well ordered, and not abuſed, as it is by the States; and that they look for at your Lordſhip's hands: it being ſtrange that the people ſhow themſelves far more careful than the governors be in all things touching the public.

" The taking of the fconces by Mr. Norris was of good moment; but now his lying before Nimeguen is greatly feared will both wafte his men, (befide the danger of the enemy, who very ftrongly marcheth that way,) and little prevail, there being a great river between him and the city. But the great fufficiency of the gentleman may overweigh other conjectures. Mr. Edward Norris delivered the companies here unto me, whom he had very well and foldierly governed, but the companies indeed very fickly and miferable. Good my Lord, hafte away, if you do come, for all things confidered I had rather you came not at all, than came not quickly; for only by your own prefence thefe courfes may be ftopped, which, if they run on, will be paft remedy. Here is Aldegonde, a man greatly fufpected, but by no man charged. He lives reftrained to his houfe, and, for aught I can find, deals with nothing, only defiring to have his caufe wholly referred to your Lordfhip, and therefore with the beft heed I can to his proceedings, I will leave him to his clearing or condemning when your Lordfhip fhall hear him. I think truly if my coming had been longer delayed, fome alteration would have followed; for the truth is, the people is weary of war, and if they do not fee fuch a courfe taken as may be likely to defend them, they will on a fudden give over the caufe. The Hollanders have newly made Count Maurice Governor of Holland and Zealand, which only grew by the delays of your Lordfhip's coming; but I cannot perceive any meaning of either diminifhing or crofling your Lordfhip's authority, but rather that the Count means wholly to depend on your Lordfhip's authority.

" With 3000*l*. charges I could find means fo to lodge myfelf and foldiers in this town, as would in an extremity command it, where now we are at their mercy. The enemy threatens divers places, as Oftend, Sluys, Bergen, and Bomel, but yet we have no certain news what he will attempt: but whatfoever it be, there is great likelihood he will endanger it: the foldiers are fo evil paid and provided of everything that is neceflary. I have dealt earneftly with the States of Zealand, for the relief of Oftend, but yet can obtain nothing but delays. To conclude, all will be loft if government be not prefently ufed. Mr. Davifon* is here very careful in her Majefty's caufes, and in your Lordfhip's; he takes

---

* William Davifon, who foon afterwards was facrificed by Elizabeth, for his fhare in the execution of Mary.

great pains therein, and goes to great charges for it. I am yet ſo new here that I cannot write ſo important matters as perhaps hereafter I ſhall, and therefore I will not any further triflingly trouble your Lordſhip, but humbly leave you to the bleſſed protection of the Almighty. At Fluſhing, this 22nd of November, 1585.

" Your Lordſhip's moſt humble

" And obedient nephew,

" PHILIP SIDNEY.

" Mr. Edward Norris, as likewiſe his brother, put great hope in your Lordſhip, which I have thought good to nouriſh, becauſe I think it fit for your Lordſhip's ſervice. Mr. Edward would fain have charge of horſes, and for cauſe will ſeek to erect a company here. I am beholding to this bearer, Captain Fenton."

Aldegonde, who is deſcribed in this letter as living in retirement at Fluſhing, had been burgo-maſter of Antwerp. His truſt in the Prince of Parma had expoſed him to the ſuſpicion of trea-chery, when he found himſelf reduced to ſurrender the city. But though his conduct ſeems to have been wanting in prudence, his character was ſuffi-ciently high to be his vindication. He was one

of the moſt eminent of the friends of William of
Orange, and his varied talents had been devoted
conſiſtently during his whole life to the Proteſtant
cauſe.   But ſince William's death the deſire for
peace, at any price, had gained ſtrength in the hearts ·
of the patriots.   The Spaniſh armies had never
been commanded by a general ſo formidable in the
field and ſo full of reſources as Alexander Farneſe,
the Prince of Parma.   His political ability was
hardly leſs eminent ; and his mercy conciliated
many whom the cruelties of Alva had made deſ-
perate. · Compared with his predeceſſors, Parma
may deſerve praiſe for clemency.   Aldegonde and
other ſtateſmen were willing to hope that a ſimilar
change for the better, whether it were enlighten-
ment or kindneſs, had come over the temper of
Philip.   At the ſame time they grew weary of
expecting efficient help from abroad.   The diſdain and bad faith with which France had met
their offer of ſovereignty had greatly depreſſed
them ; and thoſe who were inclined to the Engliſh alliance grew heart-ſick at Elizabeth's delays.

At length Leiceſter ſailed, with a brilliant train
of Engliſh peers and knights.   He was accompanied, or followed ſoon afterwards, by the Earls
of Northumberland, Oxford, and Eſſex, Lords
Sheffield,   Audley,   Willoughby,   North,   and

Burgh; and a large force of infantry and cavalry. They landed at Flushing, and Sidney escorted his uncle thence to the Hague. Passing on the way through the most populous and thriving part of Zealand and Holland, the English were astonished at the prosperous aspect of the country, and still more at the cities, which surpassed those of their own land. The general was equally surprised by the welcome with which the people greeted him. His progress resembled a triumph. The Dutch were now convinced that Elizabeth's professions were in earnest; and their own historian speaks of Leicester as having " a certain pleasant and winning majesty both in his countenance and speech,"* which gained him for a time unbounded popularity. On New Year's Day, 1586, a deputation from the States proposed to him that he should accept the office of absolute Governor-General of the Seven United Provinces, Flanders, Holland, Zealand, Utrecht, Friesland, Gelderland, and Zutphen. He had been forbidden by the Queen's private instructions to take any such office; but he eagerly grasped, nevertheless, at the dignities which were offered. His most prudent advisers, both English and Dutch,

---

* Grotius, Annals.

supported him in this courfe, in ignorance of the limits which the Queen had affigned to him. The Dutch reprefented, in ftrong terms, their need of a fupreme governor to direct the war, and hold together the various ftates. Davifon, the able ambaffador of Elizabeth, urged the fame plan, and probably it was advocated by Sidney alfo, for the Queen afterwards threw the chief blame on him. Leicefter, intoxicated with ambition and vanity, neglected to excufe his difobedience to her. She was juftly indignant, but beyond all bounds; and, in her anger, fhe propofed to take fuch violent meafures that Burleigh, though no warm friend to Leicefter, threatened to refign.* Eventually the Lord-Lieutenant was compelled to retract his pretenfions, and from thenceforward the Dutch loft confidence in him, and his authority was crippled. Elizabeth had not only been offended by the affront to her dignity. She was alfo inclined, like Aldegonde and his party in Holland, to liften creduloufly to the pacific overtures by which Philip and Parma endeavoured to delude their adverfaries and gain

---

* Motley, United Netherlands, 1. Throughout this chapter I have taken Mr. Motley's hiftory as my chief authority for the illuftration of Sidney's correfpondence.

time. Her heart was never enlifted fincerely in the caufe of the Dutch. Neither their rights, confirmed by ancient charters, nor their unparalleled fufferings, outweighed in her mind the fact that they were rebels in arms againft their fovereign. Their religion was for the moft part Calvinift, which fhe regarded with extreme averfion. Their democratic conftitution was alfo difpleafing to her. Both fhe and Leicefter felt a haughty repugnance to becoming parties to contracts of ftate with citizens. Having now taken the decifive ftep, fhe was ftill irrefolute; and the inevitable expenfe of the war almoft determined her to recede.

Meanwhile the troops were ftarving. Throughout the winter they were infufficiently provided with clothes and food, and what little they had was chiefly at the private coft of their officers. The fupplies which the Queen granted, far too fcantily and tardily, fuffered further diminution in paffing through the hands of the Army Treafurer, Lord Norris, father of the two impetuous foldiers who are named in the previous letter. Sidney wrote to Walfingham,—" The treafurer here pays our Zealand foldiers in Zealand money, which is five per cent. lofs to the poor foldiers, who, God knows, want no fuch hindrances, being fcarce able to keep life with their entire pay. If the commodity thereof be truly anſwered the Queen, yet truly is it but a poor increaſe to her Majeſty, conſidering what loſs it is to the miſerable ſoldier. But if private lucre be made, it hath too hurtful a proportion to other abuſes here." Among theſe, he found reaſon to complain that the victuallers of the army availed themſelves of friendſhip with the officers to force "the poor men to buy at a dearer rate than they might provide themſelves." One of them ſent Sidney himſelf twelve tuns of beer, with a letter claiming the right to ſerve him. "But I have refuſed," he writes, "and can aſſure you that I am better ſerved by one half by my own man's proviſion; now judge you, Sir, how poor men are dealt with." While he thus dwells with much ſympathy upon the hardſhips and wrongs of the private ſoldiers, he ſpeaks in ſtrong terms of the ſmallneſs of the force under his command, which was quite inadequate to diſcharge the duty entruſted to him. "For myſelf, I am in a garriſon as much able to command Fluſhing as the Tower is to anſwer for London, and for aught I can yet learn it is hardly to be redreſſed; for the articles intend there muſt be 5,000 kept for the defence of the country, beſide the garriſons; ſo out of them, without ſome ado, they may be hardly drawn. I mean truly, if I cannot have it helped here, to write a proteftation thereof to her Majefty and the Lords in the Council, as a thing that I can no way take on me to anfwer, if I be not increafed by, at the leaft, 400 men more than yet I have." Thefe remonftrances of Sidney's vexed the Queen, but otherwife had little effect. Men were fent, but not money, which was moft urgently wanted. The newly-arrived recruits were fcared at the gaunt and fqualid appearance of their comrades, and deferted in large numbers.

Sidney's expenfes on account of his foldiers went far beyond his means, and involved him deeply in debt. A few days after landing in Zealand he was obliged to borrow 300*l.* of a Dutch money-lender; and he wrote two months later to the general,— " I humbly befeech your Excellency, becaufe I know my lieutenant hath been at the feafide almoft this month to my great expenfe, that I may have either a quarter affigned me, or elfe that to this place they may bring fuch provifion as the increafing of the number will require. For elfe, I being not to demand pay till they be muftered, nor to be muftered till my number be complete, it will be too heavy a burden for me to bear, who, I proteft to your Excellency, am fo far from defiring gain, that I am willing to fpend all that I can make; only my care is that I may be able to go through with it to your honour and fervice, as I hope in God I fhall." In the midft of thefe anxieties we find him, as ufual, writing recommendatory letters for friends, officers, and fervants, Norris, Arundel, Williams, Morgan, and others, with the moft thoughtful intereft in their affairs. His care for the foldiers under him was not confined to their temporal wants. He took pains to educate his men, and to fee, as far as poffible, that the Queen's injunctions to the army were fulfilled by them: "that they ferved God, and demeaned themfelves religioufly."

At the beginning of February, in fpite of the difficulties with which he had .to contend, Sidney was urging his uncle to take active meafures againft the enemy. The Spaniards occupied a line which was not far from coinciding with the prefent frontier of Belgium. It advanced, however, to the north-eaft, and receded to the fouth-weft. Oftend and the whole fea-coaft to Gravelines was in the hands of the allies. In the oppofite direction the Spanifh territory extended to Nimeguen on the Waal, and Parma threatened the neighbouring city of Grave on the Meufe. But at that time he was very ill prepared to carry on hoftilities. His army was reduced to fix or eight thoufand men, troops expert in every kind of warfare, but as ill fupplied as the forces which were oppofed to them. Parma aimed for the prefent at obtaining partial fucceffes over the Englifh, luring them into ambufcades by feigned furrenders. From the following paffage this feems to have been attempted at Breda. It is part of a letter addreffed to Leicefter from Bergen-op-Zoom, where Sidney had a houfe.

" I am only to befeech your Excellency, and if I may prevail with your Excellency to perfuade you, that if the journey into Friefland be but upon fuch general grounds as they were when I came away, which may as eafily be done hereafter as now, that it will pleafe you to fend forces to the befieging of Steenberg with 2,000 of your footmen, befides them that thofe quarters may fpare, and 300 of your horfe with them here about, I will undertake upon my life either to win it, or to make the enemy raife his fiege from Grave, or, which I moft hope, both. And it fhall be done in the fight of the world, which is moft honourable and profitable. For thefe matters of practices, I affure your Excellency they are dainty in refpect of the doublenefs which almoft ever falls in them, and of the many impediments that fall in them, that if notable feafons guide not, or fome worthy perſon anſwer for it, they are better omitted than attempted. Breda, undoubtedly, at leaſt I think undoubtedly, was but a trap; for our poor Engliſhmen might have been ſuffered to take a place, which they would never have ſtriven to put them out of, till they might have cut both them and us in pieces, who ſhould come to ſeize it. But as for Graveling, I will never ſtir till I have La Motte himſelf, or ſome principal officers of his, in hand. Therefore, if it pleaſe your Excellency to let old Tutty and Read, with Sir Wm. Stanley and Sir Wm. Ruſſell, with the 300 horſe, come hither, I doubt not to ſend you honourable and comfortable news of it, for I have good underſtanding thereof, by this ſhow I made, and I know what the enemy can do ſhall not ſerve if this may be done,—500 pioneers with munition and victual according,—muſt be done; and if God will, I will do you honour in it. It grieves me very much, the ſoldiers are ſo hardly dealt with in your firſt beginning of government, not only in their pays, but in taking booties from them, as by your Excellency's letters I find. When ſoldiers begin to deſpair and to give up towns, then it is late to buy that with hundred thouſands which might have been ſaved with a trifle."

The attempt upon Steenberg was not carried

out, owing, it is faid, to a fudden thaw. A fortnight later Sidney writes again to the general :—" The enemy ftirs on every fide, and your fide muft not be idle ; for if it be, it quickly lofeth reputation. I befeech your Excellency not to be difcouraged with the Queen's difcontentments, for, the event being anything good, your glory will fhine through thefe mifts : only, if it pleafe you, to have daily counfel taken of your means, how to increafe them, and how to hufband them ; and when all is faid, if they can ferve, you fhall make a noble war ; if not, the peace is in your hand, as I find well by Aldegonde, of whom I keep a good opinion and yet a fufpicious eye." In this and fimilar paffages he betrays unconfcioufly his own fitnefs for a higher command. He prays earneftly in the fame letter that the young Count Maurice of Naffau may be fent to Flufhing, with ample authority for the redrefs of peculation and other abufes.—" I am fure he would hear advice, and I am perfuaded together we fhould do you fervices of importance. For divers things come in my way, which becaufe they belong not indeed to my charge, I am fain to let pafs. . . . There is with your Excellency Colonel Piron, one that hath ferved as well as any man in thefe parts, indeed, a moft valiant man, and of better judgment than utterance. He and

N

I have enterprifes to be done upon Flanders fide of good importance: I befeech your Excellency to difpatch him away; it fhall, I hope, turn to your fervice. . . . I am in great hope to light upon fome good occafions to do you honour and · fervice. The enterprifes are ftill hopeful, but not yet full ripe, which till they be, it were able to mar all if I fhould be far abfent. . . I will haften, as foon as I can poffibly, to your Excellency, when I have but a little fettled the matters of thefe parts, efpecially of my regiment, over whom fince it hath pleafed your Excellency to appoint me, and that they are moft joyful of it, if ever I may deferve anything of you, I humbly befeech you that they may find themfelves fo much the more tendered."

Leicefter had given to him the colonelcy of the Zealand regiment of horfe; an appointment which, popular as it was among the foldiers, did not pafs without remonftrance. Some of the veteran Dutch officers complained at being overlooked in favour of a young foreigner, who, whatever his merits, had not yet earned promotion by fervice in the field. With lefs juftice, a petition againft the nomination of foreigners was inftigated by Count Hohenlohe, or Hollock, as his name was written by the Englifh, a German nobleman. Sidney gave the following account of this to Davifon, who had returned to England :—

" Upon my having the Zealand regiment, which you know was more your perfuafion than any defire in me, the Count Hollock caufed a many-handed fupplication to be made, that no ftranger might have any regiment, but prefently after, with all the fame hands, protefted they meant it not by me, to whom they wifhed all honour, &c. The Count Maurice fhowed himfelf conftantly kind to me therein, but Mr. Paul Buys* hath too many Buffes in his head, fuch as you fhall find he will be to God and man about one pitch: happy is the conjunction with them that join in the fear of God. Medekirk far fhines above him in all matters of counfel and faithful dealing. I pray you write to me, and love me and farewell. At Flufhing, where I thank God all is well, and my garrifon in good order. This 24th of Feb. 1586."

Hohenlohe had ferved for feveral years as lieutenant-general to the Princes of Orange, with whom he was remotely connected by marriage. He was a recklefs cavalier, capable of romantic courage and generofity, but profligate, violent, and a drunkard. In all things intemperate, he

---

* Paul Buys was one of the moft able of the Dutch ftatef-men; but of bad private character, and recently oppofed to Leicefter.

was a dangerous ally; apt to be more hurtful than profitable to the caufe which he ferved, as in the fiege of Antwerp, where, after nearly refcuing the city by his valour, his folly precipitated the furrender. Such being his character, there was good reafon for omitting to give him the Zealand regiment, which he defired for himfelf; but the Queen took his part againft Sidney, whofe outfpoken. complaints of the neglect of the foldiers had put him quite out of her favour. Thereupon Hohenlohe regarded Leicefter as his enemy, and a ferious quarrel was likely to have enfued. Their reconciliation was due to Sidney, whofe genius and winning manners made the deepeft impreffion on the fiery German, and feem to have exercifed a kind of fafcination over him. Notwithftanding this and other caufes of variance, his regard for Sidney continued, and was afterwards fignally proved.

As Flufhing lay on the utmoft verge of the feat of war, Sidney paffed much of his time at Bergenop-Zoom, on the mainland. He propofed to fend for his wife thither, but was diffatisfied at the conduct of the war, and meditated fome independent plan in which, whatever it may have been, Lady Sidney could not have accompanied him. He wrote thus to his father-in-law from Utrecht,

having apparently gone to vifit Leicefter, as he
propofed in a previous letter :—

" RIGHT HONOURABLE,
" I RECEIVE divers letters from you, full of the
difcomfort which I fee, and am forry to fee, that
you daily meet with at home : and I think, fuch
is the good will it pleafeth you to bear me, that
my part of the trouble is fomething that troubles
you ; but I befeech you let it not. I had before
caft my count of danger, want, and difgrace: and,
before God, Sir, it is true in my heart, the love of
the caufe doth fo far overbalance them all, that,
with God's grace, they fhall never make me weary
of my refolution. If her Majefty were the foun-
tain, I would fear, confidering what we daily find,
that we fhould wax dry; but fhe is but a means
whom God ufeth, and I know not whether I am
deceived, but I am faithfully perfuaded, that if
fhe fhould withdraw herfelf, other fprings would
rife to help this action ; for methinks I fee the
great work indeed in hand againft the abufers of
the world, wherein it is no greater fault to have
confidence in man's power, than it is too haftily to
defpair of God's work. I think a wife and conftant man ought never to grieve while he doth
play, as a man may fay, his own part truly, tho'

others be out; but if himfelf leave his hold becaufe other mariners will be idle, he will hardly forgive himfelf his own fault. For me, I cannot promife of my own courfe, ... becaufe I know that there is a higher power that muft uphold me, or elfe I fhall fall; but certainly I truft I fhall not by other men's wants be drawn from myfelf; therefore, good Sir, to whom for my particular I am more bound than to all men befides, be not troubled with my troubles, for I have feen the worft, in my judgment, beforehand, and worfe than that cannot be.

"If the Queen pay not her foldiers fhe muft lofe her garrifons; there is no doubt thereof; but no man living fhall fay the fault is in me. What relief I can do them, I will. I will fpare no danger, if occafion ferves. I am fure no creature fhall be able to lay injuftice to my charge, and for farther doubts, truly I ftand not upon them. I have written by Adams to the Council plainly, and therefore let them determine.* It hath been a coftly beginning unto me this war, becaufe I had

---

* In fubfequent letters Sidney complains bitterly to Walfingham of the want of fupplies from home. He had previoufly difcovered great inefficiency in the Ordnance Department, for which Burleigh was cenfured by the Queen. Bourne, Memoir, pp. 447, 500-502.

nothing proportioned unto it; my fervants unexperienced, and myfelf every way unfurnifhed; but hereafter, if the war fhall continue, I fhall pafs much better through with it. For Bergen-op-Zoom, I delighted in it, I confefs, becaufe it was near the enemy; but efpecially having a very fair houfe in it, and an excellent air, I deftined it for my wife; but, finding how you deal there, and that ill payment in my abfence thence might bring forth fome mifchief, and confidering how apt the Queen is to interpret everything to my difadvantage, I have refigned it to my Lord Willoughby, my very friend, and indeed a valiant and frank gentleman, and fit for that place: therefore, I pray, you know that fo much of my regality is fallen. I underftand I am called very ambitious and proud at home; but certainly if they knew my heart they would not altogether fo judge me. I wrote to you a letter by Will, my Lord of Leicefter's jefting player, enclofed in a letter to my wife, and I never had anfwer thereof. It contained fomething to my Lord of Leicefter's, and counfel that fome way might be taken to ftay my Lady there. I fince divers times have writ, to know whether you have received them, but you never anfwered me that point. I fince find that the knave delivered the letters to my Lady of Leicefter, but whether fhe fent them you or no I know not, but earneftly defire to do, becaufe I doubt there is more interpreted thereof. . . . . We fhall have a fore war upon us this fummer, wherein if appointment had been kept, and thefe difgraces forborne, which have greatly weakened us, we had been victorious. I can fay no more at this time, but pray for your long and happy life. At Utrecht, this 24th of March, 1586.

" Your humble fon,
" PHILIP SIDNEY.

" I know not what to fay to my wife's coming till you refolve better; for if you run a ftrange courfe, I may take fuch a one here as will not be fit for any of the feminine gender.* I pray you make much of Nichol-Gery. I have been vilely deceived for armours for horfemen; if you could fpeedily fpare me any out of your armoury, I will fend them you back as foon as my own be finifhed. There was never fo good a father found a more troublefome fon. Send Sir Wm. Pelham, good Sir, and let him have Clerk's place, for we need no clerks, and it is moft neceffary to have fuch a one in the council."

---

* In a letter dated Utrecht, June 28, Sidney wrote to his father-in-law, " I am prefently going towards Flufhing, where I hear that your daughter is very well and merry." Bourne, p. 490. Lady Sidney had therefore arrived in the interval.

It appears from this letter that there was some foundation for a rumour, which had strongly excited Elizabeth's jealousy, that Lady Leicester was about to join her husband, and hold with him a sort of Court at the Hague. Her anger had since been appeased by a humble and supplicatory letter from him; but it was well that the Countess's visit did not take place. Another particular which is worth observing in this letter is the name of the bearer of Sidney's previous packet to his wife. " Will, my Lord of Leicester's jesting player," was, in all probability, one of the company of actors to which William Shakespeare belonged; for they were licensed under the title of the Earl of Leicester's servants. Nothing is known of this period of Shakespeare's life to make it unlikely that he should have been in Holland with Sidney. Such an incident would have brought the poet in sight of the cliff at Dover, which he has described so vividly, and might also have given rise to the friendship which he had afterwards with Sidney's nephew Lord Herbert. But there were two other players of the same name Will in the company; Johnson and Kemp. The latter, who was famous as a jester, fits the description best. In any case, the term " knave," applied to a young man of humble rank, would convey no reproach. The reciprocal entertainments of Leicester and the Dutch at the Hague, Amfterdam, and Utrecht, permit the conjecture that the Earl's company attended him, and performed in mafques and pantomimes.

The allied army, which had been idle too long, now commenced active hoftilities. Leicefter fent a force to the relief of Grave under John Norris, the ableft, according to Parma, of the Englifh captains, and Count Hohenlohe. The expedition was completely fuccefsful. A Spanifh detachment, which was fent to intercept the relieving army, was defeated after a fharp engagement, and 500 men, with provifions for a year, were thrown into the city. The Englifh troops had at firft wavered, and many of them fled, but their final victory made more than amends. Leicefter was thereupon extravagantly elated. The time which fhould have been ufed in improving his advantage was wafted in rejoicings. St. George's day was kept at Utrecht, with a feries of feafts and pageants, of which the general was fonder than the Queen herfelf. In the meantime Parma preffed the fiege of Grave. Hemart, the governor, overcome by the entreaties of the women, capitulated after a fhort refiftance. Leicefter was enraged at this refult of his own fupinenefs, and putting the harfheft conftruction on the young officer's mif-conduct, beheaded him with two of his lieutenants.

Sidney was now returned to Flufhing, having paffed fome time with the camp at Nimeguen. He was bufily engaged in concerting with Maurice of Naffau one of the projects which he had meditated before. Although Maurice was only nineteen years of age, he already gave indications, to Sidney's difcerning eye, of that rare military genius which afterwards made him the moft perfect general of his time. They propofed to attempt the furprife of Axel, a city in Flanders, nearly oppofite Flufhing. It was a ftrongly fortified place, commanding the dykes which protected a wide range of country to the fouth, below the level of the fea. Maurice wrote in June to the general explaining the fcheme, which he defired to be kept fecret from every one but Sidney. He appears to have received overtures from fome of the citizens, and to have proceeded very cautioufly, for fear of falling into a trap laid for him by the Spaniards. On the night of the 6th of July, 500 of the Zealand regiment under Sidney rowed acrofs the Scheld, accompanied by 500 Englifh from Bergen-op-Zoom under Lord Willoughby. On the oppofite fhore they were joined by Maurice and Colonel Piron, the fame whofe fervices had been fpecially defired by Sidney for affiftance in an enterprife upon the Flanders fide

five months before. Maurice, as governor of
Holland and Zealand, bore the chief command
in the combined force; but the actual direction
was entrusted to Sidney. He is described in
Stow's Chronicle as addressing his men at the
distance of a mile from the town, in an oration
which rests on the authority of one who served
in the war, though it has an apparent colour of
historical fiction. Something he may have said,
which is amplified to this effect: The cause they
had was God's cause, under and for whom they
fought for her Majesty, whose goodness to them
he did not need to show. They were fighting
against men of false religion, enemies to God and
His Church, against Antichrist, and against a
people whose unkindness, both in nature and in
life, was so extreme that God would not leave
them unpunished. As Englishmen, whose valour
the world feared and commended, they should
not fear death nor any peril whatever, both for
the service which they owed to their Sovereign,
and for their country's honour and their own.
He promised that no man should do any service
worth the noting, but he himself would speak to
the uttermost to prefer him to his wished purpose.
" Which oration of his," says the Chronicle,
" did so link the mind of the people, that they

chofe rather to die in that fervice, than to live
in the contrary." * They arrived at Axel at
two in the morning, marching with great order
and filence. The moat was deep; but feveral
foldiers plunged into the water with ladders, and
having fcaled the wall, opened the gates to their
comrades. The garrifon, though completely
taken by furprife, were aroufed before half the
invaders could enter, and refifted defperately.
Moft of them were flain, and the reft put to
flight. Axel was captured, with five of the
enemy's enfigns and a rich booty, without the
lofs of a fingle life to the allies. Sidney pofted
a band of picked men in the market-place for a
rallying-point in cafe of a frefh attack; while
parties marched up and down taking precautions
to fecure the city. He liberally rewarded, out
of his own purfe, the foldiers who had diftinguifhed themfelves, and returned, leaving Colonel
Piron and 800 men as a garrifon. Four neighbouring forts were obliged to furrender; and
Maurice proceeded to cut the dykes, by which,
at the next change of wind, a wide extent of the
moft fertile land in Flanders, the Pays de Waes,
was laid under water. Mondragon, a Spanifh

---

* Archer, Continuation of Stow, p. 733.

officer of eminent hardihood and fkill, was in the
neighbourhood, but unable to prevent this cataf-
trophe.   The military fuccefs of the expedition
was complete, and was generally afcribed to Sidney's conduct.   Languet had once told him that
he feared his difpofition would prove too gentle
for a commander, and that he would not be fevere
enough in difcipline.   Neceffity had, however,
braced his energies.   His firmnefs could not have
been tefted more thoroughly than in this night-
attack, which was executed on unknown ground,
with forces of different nations, and for the moft
part unpractifed in war.

While the reft of the army, lately difheartened
at the lofs of Grave, were rejoicing idly at
the capture of Axel, another adventure of a
fimilar kind offered itfelf to Sidney.   It has been
already feen from his correfpondence that information had reached him of the willingnefs of a
party in Gravelines to give up the town.   He
now heard that La Motte, the governor, would
furrender if he appeared in fufficient force.   From
his knowledge of La Motte he fufpected a ftrata-
gem.   But the foldiers, flufhed with fuccefs, were
impatient to add to their laurels, and preffed him
urgently to let them go, his lieutenant, Sir William
Brown, being one of the moft importunate.

Sidney yielded fo far as to land within a fhort diftance of Gravelines, and permitted a party which had volunteered to attempt the town, under a promife that they fhould furrender without a ufelefs fight, if they found themfelves in an ambufcade. The volunteers chofe their leader by throwing dice upon a drum-head, and the lot fell upon Sir William Brown. What Sidney had anticipated took place. Brown and his companions found themfelves entrapped by the Spaniards, who opened an irrefiftible fire from furrounding windows and cellars. A few of the Englifh efcaped: others furrendered: a few were killed. But, by Sidney's caution, what might have been a ferious difafter was averted.*

Summer was now far advanced, and the general-in-chief had done little but make preparations for taking the field. On the other fide, Parma, with inferior numbers, had ftruck many fevere blows. Since his capture of Grave he had compelled the important town of Venlo to furrender, and fubfequently ftormed Nuys on the Rhine, which was facked and burned with horrible carnage. He was now laying fiege to Rheinberg, and Leicefter proceeded to its defence with his whole army.

---

* Brooke, 135-139.

Yet the Englifh general ftill hefitated to give battle
to his redoubtable adverfary, and chofe rather to
attack Zutphen, judging rightly that Parma would
come to the fuccour of that city, and raife the fiege
of Rheinberg. It was evident that for fome time
to come the chief fcene of action would be in thofe
parts; Sidney, therefore, left Flufhing to join his
uncle. On his journey he paffed through Gertruydenberg, where Hohenlohe's quarters were.
He found the Count newly returned from a foray
with a large party of Englifh gentlemen, and
among the reft, Sir William Pelham, marfhal of
the camp, an officer of great experience and valour,
whofe arrival had been anxioufly expected by Sidney. They all fupped together at Hohenlohe's,
who, as his habit was, drank deeply. Sidney had
brought with him Edward Norris, in ignorance of
the ill-will which was borne to the family of Norris
by feveral of the company, including the Count
and Pelham. According to the prevalent fafhion,
Pelham challenged Norris to drink with him a
large goblet of wine; apparently with no friendly
intention, but in order to make him drunk. The
young man excufed himfelf on the plea of ill
health, but reluctantly complied fo far as to drain
one cup. Sir William then challenged him to
another. Angry words followed, in which Hohen-

lohe joined with coarſe ridicule. Norris, who bore
the general character of being hot-tempered and
arrogant, behaved on this occaſion with much ſelf-
control. He profeſſed his reſpect for the years
and military diſtinction of Pelham, who began to
relent towards him, with the variable humour of
a man half intoxicated. Sidney ſeized the opportunity to make peace; and the quarrel was blow-
ing over, when Hohenlohe ſilently flung the gilt
cover of a vaſe at Norris, and cut his forehead
open. Norris fell back, and the Count ſtepped
forward with his dagger drawn to kill him; but
Sidney threw his arms round Hohenlohe, and, with
the help of ſome others of the company, dragged
him out of the room.

This brutal ſcene, of which the particulars have
lately been publiſhed by Mr. Motley, from a MS.
in the State Paper Office, illuſtrates vividly but pain-
fully the manners of the time among thoſe with
whom Sidney's life was paſſed. Such exceſſes may
have been rare, but it is evident that the tone of
ſociety did not give any ſecurity againſt them.
The gueſts at this ſupper were no vulgar brawlers,
but ſome of the moſt illuſtrious noblemen and
gentlemen of both countries. It is not wonderful that when outrages ſo violent were poſſible
among counts and earls, the beſt men ſhould inſiſt

superstitiously on military honour, and magnify the laws of chivalry.   But it would be a great error to judge of those rough warriors merely by the particulars in which their behaviour is unfit to compare with that of our own day.   Manners, though they are the most obvious characteristics of a nation or an individual, are also the most superficial.   They are the last points to be affected by true civilization, the progress of which is from the heart outwards to the demeanour and language, and the ease with which they are imitated makes them very fallacious as a sign of real worth. Viewed apart from the prejudice which their coarseness of behaviour and speech excites, the gentlemen of Elizabeth's day were, as a class, worthy rivals of the best which subsequent generations have seen; whether we regard their Christian faith, their public spirit, their intellectual vigour and culture, or their frankness and courtesy of heart.   Of the vice of intemperance it is asserted by an old writer * that it first became general in England through these wars, being learned from the Dutch and Germans in the moist climate of the Netherlands.   It is probably with reason that Sidney's friends claim for him a large share in

---

* Camden ; quoted by Zouch, p. 242.

leading the fashion, both of the Court and of the camp, to purer and nobler pleasures. The next reign exhibited a strange rivalry between literature and philosophy, in their brightest splendour, on the one hand; and, on the other, the infamy of drunkenness among the highest Court ladies.

Edward Norris escaped from Gertruydenberg, where his life was hardly safe among the soldiers of Hohenlohe, and sent him a challenge to mortal combat soon afterwards. The message was borne by Sidney, who exposed himself to some peril in standing forth almost alone as Norris's friend. But the duel never took place, being postponed by the rapid succession of events. On August 28th, Leicester held a review of his army, which amounted to 5,000 English and Irish infantry and 1,400 cavalry, besides about 2,000 Dutch and German troops. Two days later he invested Doesburg, a place of moderate strength, which lay upon the road to Zutphen. The English leaders were all present. Sir William Pelham directed the siege operations, and received a wound, which, for a few days, was thought dangerous. Sir John Norris, who had been recently knighted for his conduct in the relief of Grave, commanded the infantry. The highspirited young Earl of Essex, though a boy in years, was in command of the cavalry. He now ferved in the fiege as a volunteer. Sir Thomas Cecil, the governor of Brill, had left his fecure poft, like Sidney, to fhare in the dangers and glory of the field. Sidney's brother Robert was alfo prefent, as he had been wherever he could meet the enemy. His conduct was worthy of his kindred, and earned him the fpurs of knighthood fhortly afterwards. The allies opened fire with nine or ten pieces of ordnance, and foon had made two breaches, practicable for affault. Hohenlohe led one party, Sir John Norris the other; and they were both on the point of advancing to the attack when Doefburg furrendered. The garrifon ftipulated only for their own lives, and left the city at Leicefter's difpofal. Orders were given that the property of the citizens fhould be refpected, and that no one fhould be fubject to ill ufage; yet Effex and other chief officers were compelled to interfere with blows to ftop the foldiers from facking the town. The troops of England in the Netherlands had long before this time acquired a fhameful notoriety for plunder and infubordination.*

From Doefburg to Zutphen is about a day's march. Leicefter advanced without lofs of time,

---

* Languet's Letters. Pears, p. 176.

and took up pofitions for the fiege of the latter place, the capital of the ancient county of Zutphen. It was a well-built and ftrongly-fortified city, on the right bank of the Yffel, which there flows northward, in a broad ftream, through a plain of feemingly boundlefs extent. The allied army began to entrench themfelves on both fides of the river. On the right fide, a hill in a commanding fituation was occupied by Sir John Norris, with whom were Count Lewis William of Naffau and Sidney. The general himfelf croffed over by a bridge of boats which he had conftructed, and prepared to attack fome ftrong fconces or outworks, on the left bank, which formed a material defence of the city. While the allied army was engaged in throwing up entrenchments, the Prince of Parma, having raifed the fiege of Rheinberg, came in hafte to reconnoitre their pofition. By paffing clofe under a fort which Leicefter had abandoned immediately before, he fucceeded in entering Zutphen. His firft thought was to remain and defend the city himfelf, for he faw that the allied pofitions were very ftrong. Yielding, it is faid,* to the confidence expreffed by his lieutenant Verdugo, he left him in command; but took meafures to re-

* Strada.

lieve Zutphen at once by fending a large convoy of wheat and other fupplies. Provifions were collected with the utmoft rapidity and fecrefy. Only one road, however, was practicable for conveying them, and that lay not far to the eaft of Sir John Norris's camp. Parma was not able to conceal his vaft preparations altogether; and Leicefter received intelligence of the time when the fupplies were to be expected. He gave orders accordingly to Sir William Stanley, with 300 pikemen, and Sir John Norris, with 200 horfe, to intercept the convoy on its road.

On the morning of the 22nd of September they ftarted before daybreak for the little village of Warnsfeld, about a mile from the city. The expedition was joined by about fifty volunteers, the flower of the Englifh army, who galloped, unawares to the general, to take part in the expected fkirmifh. Among thefe were Effex, Audley, Willoughby, Pelham, Ruffell, and the two Sidneys, with their efquires. When the horfemen, who had preffed forward in advance, arrived at the village, there was fo thick a fog that a man could not be feen ten paces off. They had no fcouts, and were quite ignorant of the enemy's ftrength. Prefently they heard the found of the waggons approaching; and on a fudden the fog cleared away,

and fhowed them a Spanifh army lining both fides
of the road, and intrenched in the churchyard of
Warnsfeld. The enemy was about 3000 ftrong,
according to the report which Parma gave afterwards to the king of Spain. They were a mixed
force of Spaniards, Italians, and Albanians, under
the command of the Marquis of Guafto, who was
in front, fupported by many diftinguifhed noblemen and captains, at the head of a fquadron of
mounted arquebufiers. It was evident that the
Englifh had fallen themfelves into an ambufcade
in the act of laying one. Retreat was ftill poffible ; but they did not hefitate to attack the over-
whelming numbers oppofed them. Effex cried,
" For the honour of England, my fellows, follow
me," and rode forward at a gallop. Sidney and
the others accompanied him, and charged with
lance in reft. Then, throwing afide their lances,
they took to their curtle-axes, and plied them fo
furioufly that the enemy's horfe fell back, and
rallied behind the line of pikemen. The brave
Lord Willoughby, whofe " ftout behaviour," and
" courage fierce and fell," is the theme of a ftir-
ring old Englifh ballad, overthrew the leader of
the Albanian cavalry, and dafhing on, without
paufing to accept his furrender, found himfelf
alone in the midft of the enemy. Some of them

caught hold of his trappings, and tore them off in the effort to take him prifoner; in which they would have fucceeded, had not Sidney and others come to the refcue. Many more fuch inftances of recklefs valour are related. Sir William Perrott, a reputed grandfon of King Henry VIII, killed in fingle combat Count Hannibal Gonzaga, the commander of the Italians. Lord North, who had been invalided with a wound in the leg, rofe from his bed to join the battle, with only one boot on. The fight refembled in character the brilliant and difaftrous fkirmifh of Balaklava in our own day. It was a magnificent difplay of courage, which had been long pent up in forced inaction, and was now exhibited in a manner contrary to the fcience of war. Again and again the Englifh cavalry broke through their adverfaries' line, only to find beyond them an army drawn up in pofition, and to receive volleys of mufketry, and even of cannon; for the battle extended within range of the guns of Zutphen.

Sidney had been warned by Languet, in cafe he fhould go into the Netherlands, to beware of this very reckleffnefs. "Do not," faid his friend, in a letter written eight years before, "give the glorious name of courage to a fault which only feems to have fomething in common with it. It

is the folly of our age, that moſt men of high
birth think it more honourable to do the work
of a ſoldier than of a leader, and would rather
earn a name for boldneſs than for judgment.
Hence in our countries we can ſcarcely find a veteran commander, and this is owing ſimply to our
raſhneſs." Languet's cenſure was applicable to
the conduct of the whole body of Engliſh knights
on this day, but peculiarly to that of Sidney himſelf. He had come to the fight without leave,
and holding no command, his ſquadron of horſe
having been ſent to guard the city of Deventer.
On his way to the field he had met Sir William
Pelham, recovered from his wound, and finding
him, as it happened, without leg armour, had
caſt aſide his own cuiſſes in a fit of romantic
emulation. Thus unprotected, he charged with
Eſſex, Willoughby, and the reſt; and his behaviour, conſpicuous even among ſo many heroes,
excited the admiration both of friends and foes.
At the ſecond charge his horſe was ſhot under
him; but he immediately mounted another, and
was again in the thickeſt of the battle. In the
next encounter he charged right through the
enemy's ranks, and came upon their entrenchments. At that moment a muſket-ball hit him
on the thigh, a little above the knee, where he
ſhould have been defended by the cuiſſes which

he had taken off. The ball fhattered the bone, inflicting a hideous wound, and penetrated upwards into his leg. Yet Sidney endeavoured to charge once more. His horfe, however, was reftive, and unaccuftomed to his rider, who was unable now to manage him. Unwillingly, he returned to the camp, a mile and a-half diftant, fuffering intenfe pain, but refufing the aid of the fquire who offered to lead his horfe.

It was on his way that the incident occurred which more than any other is affociated with his name. We may beft repeat the often-quoted words in which Lord Brooke has defcribed his friend's gentle charity :—" Paffing along the reft of the army where his uncle the general was, and being thirfty with excefs of bleeding, he called for drink, which was prefently brought him ; but as he was putting the bottle to his mouth, he faw a foot-foldier carried along, who had eaten his laft at the fame feaft, ghaftly cafting up his eyes at the bottle ; which Sir Philip perceiving, took it from his head before he drank, and delivered it to the poor man, with thefe words, *Thy neceffity is yet greater than mine.*" The foldier having drunk, Sidney pledged him in the remainder of the draught.*

---

* Brooke, 146.

He was met by his uncle, who had croffed the river to obferve the engagement, with a large force. " O Philip !" cried Leicefter, " I am forry to fee thy hurt." " O my lord !" he anfwered, " this have I done to do you honour, and her Majefty fome fervice." Then Sir William Ruffell came up bloody from the fight, where he had been wielding his curtle-axe to the wonder and terror of the enemy. At the fight of Sidney's condition he wept like a child, exclaiming, " O noble Sir Philip ! there was never man attained hurt more honourably than you have done, nor any ferved like unto you." Sidney faid with refignation, " God directed the bullet ;" and he bade the furgeons probe his wound without delay, and thoroughly, while he had ftill ftrength to bear the pain. They were unable to extract the bullet, but they fet the bone ; and he was fent in a precarious ftate to Arnheim, where Leicefter had lately refided. The Earl wrote to England on the following day, " How God will difpofe of him, I know not, but fear I muft needs greatly the worft ; the blow in fo dangerous a place and fo great ; yet did I never hear of any man that did abide the dreffing and fetting his bones better than he did, and he was carried afterwards in my barge to Arnheim, and I hear this day he is ftill of good heart, and comforteth all about him as much as may be. God of His mercy grant him his life, which I cannot but doubt of greatly. I was abroad at that time in the field, giving fome order to fupply that bufinefs, which did endure almoft two hours in continual fight, and meeting Philip coming upon his horfe-back, not a little to my grief. But I would you had ftood by to hear his moft loyal fpeeches to her Majefty; his conftant mind to the caufe, his loving care over me, and his moft refolute determination for death, not a jot appalled for his blow, which is the moft grievous that ever I faw with fuch a bullet; riding fo long, a mile and a-half, upon his horfe, ere he came to the camp; not ceafing to fpeak ftill of her Majefty; being glad if his hurt and death might any way honour her: for hers he was whilft he lived, and God's he was fure to be if he died; praying all men to think that the caufe was as well her Majefty's as the country's; and not to be difcouraged, ' for you have feen fuch fuccefs as may encourage us all; and this my hurt is the ordinance of God by the hap of the war.' "

Sidney's fatal wound has made the battle of Zutphen more celebrated than it would otherwife have been. It was an indecifive engagement of

lefs than two hours, in which, while much glory
was won by the Englifh, the real advantage remained with the enemy. Leicefter hefitated to
give orders for a general advance of his army;
and the detachment, unfupported, was unable to
hinder Parma's fupplies and reinforcements from
entering the city. The Spanifh mufketeers made
their way on gradually, leading the waggon horfes
as they fought; and thus, as their own hiftorian
defcribes,* like a boat rowing hard into port
againft the wind, with fluctuating progrefs they
accomplifhed their purpofe. Yet the battle was
long remembered as one of extraordinary fierce-
nefs. Its effect was greatly to abate the dread
in which the Spaniards were held. A fplendid
proof had been given that they were not invin-
cible. Three fucceffive times the Englifh knights
had charged and broken a body which is efti-
mated at fivefold their own number. Several of
the chief captains on the Spanifh fide had fallen,
and the Marquis of Guafto narrowly efcaped with
his life. Nor was the battle without other fpecial
circumftances of intereft. George Crefcia, the
Albanian chief, who had been unhorfed by Lord
Willoughby, yielded himfelf his prifoner volun-

---

* Strada.

tarily, after refuſing to ſurrender to any other. Sir John Norris, who had quarrelled with Sir William Stanley, cried, " Let us be friends together this day, and die ſide by ſide, if need be, in her Majeſty's cauſe ;" and Stanley anſwered, " Living or dying, I will ſtand or lie by you in friendſhip."

CHAPTER VII.

SIDNEY'S DEATH.

" What hath he loft, that fuch great grace hath won?
  Young years for endlefs years, and hope unfure
Of fortune's gifts, for wealth that ftill fhall dure.
  O happy race, with fo great praifes run!"
                                SIR WALTER RALEIGH.

N extreme danger, but in good heart, Sidney was conveyed in Leicefter's barge to Arnheim, paft burnt villages, ruined abbeys, and devaftated plains. The fituation of the city was healthy and pleafant, on the banks of the Rhine, in what is called the Paradife of Holland, though now, through the ravages of war, wearing another afpect. There he was joined by his wife, who had croffed over to the Netherlands, not long after his letter to Walfingham of March 24. She nurfed him anxioufly, with affiduous watchfulnefs, which

indeed his wound required. Her comfort was
the more neceffary, as his illnefs was aggravated
by grief of mind. He was mourning for the
recent lofs of both his parents. Sir Henry Sidney
had died at Ludlow in the previous May, bearing
with him to the grave the refpect of all who knew
him. Three months later his widow breathed
her laft, dying in the fame gentle and Chriftian
fpirit in which fhe had lived. "During the
whole courfe of her ficknefs, and efpecially a little
before it pleafed God to call her to His mercy,
fhe ufed fuch godly fpeeches, earneft and effectual
perfuafives to all about her . . . . as inwardly
pierced the hearts of many that heard her.
Though they before knew her to exceed moft of
her fex in fingular virtue and quality, good fpeech,
apt and ready conception, excellency of wit, and
notable delivery, yet her difcourfe then amazed
and aftonifhed the hearers."* The news of her
death was probably ftill frefh to her fon. None
of his letters relating to this time have been preferved; but the depth of his forrow may be efti-
mated by the trueft meafure, his devoted love to
his parents when living. He had been a dutiful
fon; and there is no feature in his character

---

* Molyneux, in Holinfhed.

more clearly marked than tender family affection.

Whatever confolation he could have from the fondnefs of his wife, or from the fympathy of friends, was abundantly forthcoming. If condolence and kindnefs, together with the beft medical fkill of the time, could have faved his life, he would have done well. As foon as the particulars of the battle of Zutphen were known in England, Sidney's health became a matter of public anxiety. The Queen difmiffed at once the prejudice which fhe had lately entertained againft him, and affured him of her friendfhip with her own hand. She wrote a letter to cheer him, inquiring how he was, and defiring that daily reports fhould be fent to her. Count Hohenlohe, lying feverely wounded in the face, fent to him a famous phyfician, who was in attendance on himfelf, with generofity refembling Sidney's own. The opinion of this doctor, Adrian van der Spiegel, was unfavourable to Sidney's recovery. He foon became delirious, and for feveral days he lay between life and death. Then fome figns of amendment appeared. Leicefter, who left the camp to vifit him at the firft opportunity, wrote home on September 27,* " The furgeons have very good hope

---

* MS. State Paper Office; Holland Correfpondence, vol. xxxv.

P

of him ;" and again, ten days after the battle, "All the worſt days be paſt, as both ſurgeons and phyſicians have informed me, and he amends as well as is poſſible in this time, and himſelf finds it, for he ſleeps and reſts well, and hath a good ſtomach to eat, without fear or any diſtemper at all. I thank God for it." But his deſcription ſeems to have been coloured by his own ſanguine temper, which was apt to imagine things as he deſired them to be. Leiceſter's veracity can never be depended on, where his wiſhes or intereſts are concerned. The caſe warranted no ſuch hopes as thoſe with which he buoyed up his own ſpirits, and thoſe of the Engliſh nation. With the ſtrongeſt conſtitution, Sidney's recovery would have been doubtful; and unhappily he was far leſs robuſt than might have been expected from his well-proportioned and athletic frame.

He never doubted for himſelf that he was on his death-bed; and he looked death ſteadily in the face. The Calviniſt divines, who came to inſtruct him, found him better qualified to teach than to learn of them. Calling to his bedſide the miniſters of both nations who viſited him, he profeſſed before them his Chriſtian faith, and invited them to pray in company with him, and ſuffer him to lead them. "For," he ſaid, "the

fecret fins of his heart were beft known to himfelf,
and he therefore more properly inftructed how
to apply to himfelf the facrifice of our Saviour's
paffion and merits."* He proceeded to pray
aloud, and they followed him, choked with fighs
and tears. After a time he defifted fuddenly,
and began immediately to confult them as to the
teftimony of the heathen concerning the immortality of the foul, and the confirmation which it
received from the Old and New Teftaments.
One of his former fayings was, " He cannot be
good, who knows not why he is good ;" and, confiftently with this opinion, he had given much
time to the ftudy of Chriftian evidences. He
had commenced a tranflation of the great treatife,
" On the Truenefs of the Chriftian Religion," of
his friend Mornay, " the Pope of the Huguenots,"
as he was called.† In this book we may expect
to find the principles of Sidney's religion, efpecially confidering the author's clofe alliance and
friendfhip with Languet. Judging thus, Sidney's
faith appears to have been of that enlightened kind

---

* Brooke, p. 152.

† This work was completed at his requeft by A. Golding,
after his death. Another unfinifhed work of Sidney's was
a tranflation of Du Bartas' once celebrated poem on the
Creation. Collier, Life of Spenfer.

which holds Chriftianity as the fupreme Philofophy, no lefs than the fupreme Religion. The book is free from the morbid prominence of fingle doctrines which is the common refult of controverfy. Mornay ftates clearly and impreffively the cardinal points of the Gofpel: the unity of God; the myftery of the Trinity; the immortality of the foul; the corruption of human nature; that God himfelf is the "fovereign welfare of man;" the call of Ifrael; the truth of Scripture; and the mediation of Chrift. The handling of the treatife differs from that of fimilar modern works. It is written to confirm believers rather than to convince fceptics, and therefore lays more ftrefs upon doctrines than upon arguments. The arguments, too, are partly abftract reafonings from the affumed nature of things, and partly appeals to the authority of ancient philofophers, whofe writings, together with thofe of the early doctors of the Church, are cited with copious learning in fupport of revelation. The opinions which prevailed at that time, concerning the beft of the heathens, were fomewhat contradictory. While their religion was fet at nought as devilifh, their philofophical fpeculations were efteemed as hardly lefs than infallible. Sidney held the wifdom of Plato in efpecial veneration; and during his illnefs he delighted much in converfing with his friends upon thofe intimations of eternity which pervade his dialogues. It feems worth while to dwell upon thefe records of the inward fprings of Sidney's life. Nor does there appear to be any fufficient caufe for refraining from the contemplation. No nobler object is prefented by this world than a dying Chriftian's mind; in which, more than in hiftory or in poetry, we may trace the elements of that unattained ideal which we call a man's better felf: while time mellows whatever reminifcences are inharmonious, and wins belief for more lovelinefs and fublimity in human character than even the moft perfect lives exhibit confiftently.

Gifford, one of Leicefter's Englifh chaplains, has left a minute account of Sidney's laft days, in which he writes:—"Although he had profeffed the Gofpel, loved and favoured thofe that did embrace it, entered deeply into the concerns of the Church, taken good order and very good care for his family and foldiers to be inftructed, and to be brought to live accordingly, yet entering into deeper examination of his life now in the time of his affliction, he was moved to deep forrow." Sidney contrafted his own life with thofe of good men in Scripture, who were fuftained under tribulation by the remembrance of having glorified God. "It is not fo in me," he faid, "my life has been vain, vain, vain." He was uneafy in confcience with regard to his Arcadia, and, after confultation with the minifters, expreffed his defire that it fhould be burned.* He complained feveral times "that his mind was dull in prayer, and that his thoughts did not afcend up fo quickly as he defired. For having before in manful fort entreated the Lord with fervent prayer, he thought he fhould at all times feel that fervency, and was grieved when he found any thought interrupting the fame." At another time, after lying filent, he broke forth fuddenly into incoherent words, expreffing "his fenfe of the wretchednefs of man, 'a poor worm,' of the mercies of God, and of his merciful providence; and this he did with vehement geftures and great joy, even ravifhed with the confideration of God's omnipotency, providence, and goodnefs, whofe fatherly love in remembering to chaften him he now felt, adding, how unfearchable the myfteries of God's Word are."† He thanked God for having allowed him

---

* Brooke, p. 19.

† Gifford's Narrative, printed by Zouch, Memoirs, pp. 267-277.

ſpace for repentance. At another time the proſpect of his poſſible recovery flaſhed through his
mind, and he declared, " I have vowed my life to
God."

He took an early opportunity to make his will.
By the recent death of his father he had become
poſſeſſed of a conſiderable fortune ; but the debts
which he had incurred for the ſake of the naked
and hungry ſoldiers of Fluſhing, together with his
own profuſe expenſe, had encumbered his eſtate
far more than he ſuſpected. His will was worded
in the pious ancient mode :—" I, Sir Philip Sidney, Kt., ſore wounded in body, but whole in mind,
all praiſes be to God, do make this my laſt Will
and Teſtament in manner and form following :
Firſt, I bequeath my ſoul to Almighty God who
gave it me, and my body to the duſt from whence
it came." He proceeded to leave half his property to his " moſt dear and loving wife, Dame
Frances Sidney," for her lifetime ; and he alſo
made her his ſole executrix. To his daughter he
left 4,000 crowns, to be put to the beſt inveſtment
in London or the Netherlands, but not " in any
caſe to be let out to any uſury at all." He gave
directions that his debts ſhould be paid ; and bequeathed almoſt innumerable legacies to friends of
every ſtation. The bulk of his property he left

to his brothers, Robert and Thomas,* referving the life intereft in half, which he had given to his wife.

Having difcharged this duty, he indulged his fancy by turning his misfortune to a theme of poetry, and wrote a fong upon his wounded thigh, of which only the title is preferved, *La Cuiſſe Rompue.* This fong he caufed to be fet to mufic, and fung to him. Through pain and forrow his mind preferved the fame brilliant vivacity which had made him formerly the jewel of the Court; and his perfect ingenuoufnefs led him to manifeft each varying phafe of his foul without a fhadow of that fear of the world's criticifm which befets common minds.

· He fuffered much, and bore his fufferings with ferene patience. From conftant lying his fhoulder-blades wore through his delicate fkin. Meanwhile he became weaker and weaker. His wife, almoft exhaufted with anxious watching, looked vainly for any hopeful fymptom. One day his fine fenfe perceived that mortification had fet in, before his attendants were aware of the change. He blufhed at the offence which his condition might give to them, but calmly recognized the fure prefage of death, and fpoke of his approaching end with

---

* In page 10, Sidney's youngeft brother is mifcalled William.

compofure, faying " he feared not to die, but he was afraid left the pangs of death fhould be fo grievous that he might lofe his underftanding."

On the evening of the 16th of October he was in great pain, and wrote to Wier, a phyfician of Cleves :—

" My Wier, come, come : my life is in danger, and I want you. I will not be ungrateful, living or dead. I cannot write more, but befeech you to make hafte." *

The fame night, as it drew towards morning, Gifford inquired of Sidney how he did. " I feel myfelf more weak," he anfwered. " I truft," faid Gifford, " you are thoroughly prepared for death, if God fhall call you." At this Sidney made a little paufe, and then rejoined, " I have a doubt : pray refolve me in it. I have not flept this night. I have very earneftly and humbly befought the Lord to give me fome fleep. He hath denied it : this caufeth me to doubt that God doth not regard me, nor hear any of my prayers. This doth trouble me." The chaplain's explanation was, " that for matters touching falvation or pardon of

---

* The original, in Latin, written in a tremulous hand, is in the State Paper Office, accompanied by a letter from Wier's nephew, defcribing Sidney's condition.

fin through Chrift, He gave an abfolute promife:
but for things concerning this life, God hath promifed them but with caution. What He hath
abfolutely promifed we may affuredly look to receive; craving in faith that which He hath thus
promifed." Sidney accepted the diftinction:—" I
am fully fatisfied and refolved with this anfwer:
no doubt it is even fo; then I will fubmit myfelf
to His will in thefe outward things." Prefently
he fpoke again: "I had this night a trouble in
my mind; for, fearching myfelf, methought I had
not a full and fure hold of Chrift. After I had
continued in this perplexity awhile, how ftrangely
God did deliver me! for it was a ftrange deliver-
ance which I had. There came to my remembrance a vanity in which I delighted, whereof I had
not rid myfelf. I rid myfelf of it, and prefently
my joy and comfort returned." A few hours
after, putting out his hand to Gifford, and "flap-
ping him gently on the cheek," he faid, "I would
not change my joy for the empire of the world."
Then he afked to be fpoken to out of the Scrip-
tures, which was accordingly continued, 'for the
fpace of three or four hours. Once or twice the
readers paufed, fuppofing him to be afleep; but
he faid immediately, "I pray you fpeak unto me
ftill."

Later in the day he roufed himfelf, to add a codicil to his will. This was chiefly for the pur-pofe of giving prefents and memorials to thofe who had attended upon him during his illnefs; his attached fecretary William Temple, the chaplains, phyficians, and others. Now, too, he parted with the laft poffeffions that bound him to human glory. He left his beft fword to the Earl of Effex, and his fecond to Lord Willoughby.

His friends came in to take their leave of him; laft of all his dear brother Robert. With the heavenly firmnefs of a dying Chriftian, Philip calmed his brother's paffionate grief, and gave to him his final injunctions,—" Love my memory; cherifh my friends; their faith to me may affure you they are honeft: but above all, govern your will and affections by the will and Word of your Creator, in me beholding the end of this world with all her vanities." In thefe words he bade him farewell; but Robert clung to him weeping and fobbing, unable to control his forrow. At length Philip bade his friends to lead his brother away.*

He fpoke no more, and foon afterwards ap-peared to be infenfible. Temple and Gifford

---

* Brooke, p. 160. Gifford, in Zouch, p. 275.

were with him to the laſt. Gifford begged him to give a ſign, if he was ſtill conſcious:—" Sir, if you hear what I ſay, let us by ſome means know it ; and if you have ſtill your inward joy and con-ſolation in God, hold up your hand." At theſe words the dying man lifted up his hand, which they thought he could ſcarcely have moved, and ſtretched it out high above his head. His friends cried aloud with joy. After this he raiſed both his hands, and ſet them together on his breaſt, holding them upwards in an attitude of prayer. In that poſture they remained until they grew cold and ſtiff.

He paſſed from this world on the 17th of October, according to the old ſtyle of the calendar, which was then uſed. In ſix more weeks he would have completed his thirty-ſecond year.

The news of Sir Philip Sidney's death was re-ceived in England as a national calamity. A public mourning was made for him, a thing unprecedented in the caſe of a private individual. " For many months," his firſt editor ſtates, " it was counted indecent for any gentleman of quality to appear, at Court or in the city, in light or gaudy apparel." Elizabeth was ſo deeply moved, that, in writing to Leiceſter, ſhe forgot a great part of her inſtruc-tions, which ſhe was obliged to deſpatch afterwards by a fecond meffenger. Walfingham was unable for a time to attend to public bufinefs. The excellent Lord Buckhurft declared that no man had ever more tears at his death. Mornay wrote from France, " I bewail his lofs not for England only, but for all Chriftendom. The Almighty has envied us the poffeffion of him, judging him perhaps worthy of a better world." Leicefter, whofe felfifhnefs and many vices were foftened by his impulfive warmth of feeling, lamented his lofs as if he had been his own fon. He was with Sir Philip on the day of his death, and he had no fpirit for the war afterwards. For Sidney had not only been, as he faid, the " greateft comfort" to him, but his fervices had been invaluable as a counfellor and peacemaker. At firft Leicefter had undervalued his nephew's qualities, regarding him as an accomplifhed but fomewhat forward young man. Nor is it likely that he ever appreciated him worthily. But he found reafon to acknowledge that his own authority had been mainly upheld by Sidney, who did much to conciliate the Earl's many adverfaries. It was indeed believed that Sidney might have afpired, if he had chofen, to his uncle's place of Governor-General, with the good-will of the United Provinces. They now contended with England for his obfequies.

Elizabeth was petitioned by the States of Zealand that they might have the honour of burying him at the expenfe of their government. They promifed to erect him as fair a monument as any prince in Chriftendom had. But the Queen refufed, and determined to order his funeral at her own coft. His corpfe was brought from Arnheim to Flufhing, and there put on board a pinnace of his own, hung with black drapery and efcutcheons. At the embarkation the whole garrifon marched down to the feafide trailing their enfigns, and followed by the citizens in long proceffion. The veffel, faluted on its departure with a triple difcharge of cannon and mufketry, proceeded with a calm voyage acrofs the German Ocean and up the Thames. At the Tower ftairs the corpfe was landed, and lay in ftate at the Minories for four months, while preparations were made on a grand fcale for the funeral.

While Sidney's unburied corpfe was ftill awaiting interment, an hiftorical event occurred which has given rife to a ftrange tale in his honour. The throne of Poland fell vacant; and among the numerous candidates from different nations who afpired to be elected, Sir Philip Sidney was afterwards faid to have been put in nomination. Tradition went fo far as to give reafons why he was not elected, Sir Robert Naunton * imputing oppofition to Elizabeth, who could not endure to fee " her fheep marked with a foreign mark :" while, on the other hand, the learned Fuller † defcribes Sidney himfelf as " preferring rather to be a fubject of Queen Elizabeth than a fovereign beyond the feas." In fact, however, the death of Sidney preceded by more than a month that of King Stephen, which took place at Grodno, in December, 1586, after a profperous reign of twelve years.‡ The ftory, though often repeated fince without queftion, is only valuable as betraying the high conceptions which Sidney's countrymen formed of him, and poffibly fome vague difcourfe of what he might have been if he had lived. The late king was not of royal birth, and had proved the beft of all the Polifh fovereigns. In the previous interregnum Sidney had vifited Poland as a youth of twenty, and had fince taken fpecial intereft in the politics of the kingdom. Thefe circumftances, together with Sidney's rare accomplifhments, probably fuggefted this tale, which would be hard to believe, even if it were confiftent with dates.

---

* Naunton's Regalia.   † Fuller's Worthies.
‡ L'Art de vérifier les Dates.

His funeral took place in St. Paul's Cathedral, on the 16th of February, 1587, with much ftate.* The proceffion paffed in a long line through the city from the Minories. It was led by thirty-two poor men, anfwering to the years of his age. Then came a group of friends, among whom Sir Francis Drake is named. No part of the melancholy ceremonial which is cuftomary in attending a foldier to his grave was wanting on this occafion. One page led the dead knight's horfe, another bore his broken lance. Five heralds carried feverally his gilt fpurs of knighthood, his gauntlets, his helmet and creft, his fhield, and his coat-of-arms. The pall was borne by four young men, the deareft among his friends; Fulke Greville, Edward Dyer, Edward Wotton, and Thomas Dudley. Robert Sidney followed as chief mourner. With him were Thomas Sidney, the Earls of Huntingdon, Pembroke, Leicefter, and Effex, and Lords Willoughby and North. The Seven United Provinces fent each their reprefentative. The Lord Mayor and Aldermen of London followed, with the Liverymen of the Grocers' Company, to which Sidney had belonged. A large body of mufketeers,

---

* A curious narrative of Sidney's death and funeral is printed at the end of this volume.

pikemen, and halberdiers, brought up the rear of the proceffion.*

No monument is known to have been erected over his grave; but a wooden tablet, with a bombaftic infcription, imitated from a French epigram on another perfon, was attached to one of the pillars of the cathedral, and doubtlefs perifhed in the Great Fire. The precife fpot which contains Sidney's duft is uncertain. It was, however, under the Lady Chapel, at the back of the high altar of old St. Paul's.

To the great diftrefs of Walfingham, who was his executor, it was found impoffible to carry out the intentions of his will. Sidney's perfonal property was not fufficient to difcharge a third part of his debts, and the lawyers who were confulted on the fubject gave their opinion that the will contained no provifion for the fale of landed eftates for this purpofe. " It doth greatly afflict me," wrote Walfingham, " that a gentleman who hath lived fo unfpotted in reputation, and had fo great care to fee all men fatisfied, fhould be fo expofed to the outcry of his creditors."† He paid

---

* An illuftrated account of Sidney's funeral is exhibited in the King's Library of the Britifh Mufeum.

† Bruce's Leicefter Correfpondence.

out of his own purſe 6,000*l.*, which he could ill afford, for the diſcharge of his ſon-in-law's liabilities. His daughter was at firſt overwhelmed with care and ſorrow for her loſs. For ſome weeks ſhe remained at Utrecht, too ill to return to England. In December ſhe bore a dead child, and for a long time her life was in ſerious danger. She recovered, however, and lived to ſee another huſband taken from her by a violent death, an objeƈt of popular ſympathy, equally ſtrong, though far leſs worthy. Her ſecond huſband was Robert Devereux, Earl of Eſſex. After his execution ſhe joined the Roman Catholic religion. Some years later ſhe was married a third time, to the Earl of Clanricarde.

Elizabeth Sidney, Sir Philip's only daughter, who received from the Queen her own name, was married to the Earl of Rutland, and died at the age of thirty, without iſſue.

It is delightful to turn from theſe ſequels of Sidney's life, which are not without ſadneſs, as ſeeming to efface his bright remembrance from the world, to review the elegies which were written in his memory. The admiration and ſorrow of the Engliſh people found utterance in poetry more copious and tender, perhaps, than has ever been poured forth in lamentation for any man's death in any nation. Oxford and Cambridge publifhed three volumes of Latin elegiac verfe, entitled " Lachrymæ," of which two volumes were contributed by the former univerfity. King James of Scotland, by whom, in one of his laft letters, Sidney had defired to be held in affectionate remembrance,* fhowed his efteem for his deceafed friend by Sonnets, of indifferent merit, both in Englifh and Latin. To recite even the names of the authors, who have celebrated Sidney's praifes in profe and verfe, would be tedious; for the lift, it is faid, might without difficulty be extended beyond 200. It includes the names of the Countefs of Pembroke, of Spenfer, Sir Walter Raleigh, Ben Jonfon, Waller, among the poets of his own and of the next generation, befide others of lefs note. Young, Cowper, Shelley, and Southey, in modern times, have fwelled the catalogue of poets; while of the hiftorians of the politics or literature of Elizabeth's reign, almoft every one has paufed to commemorate Sidney's excellence. Some have touched upon his name with paffing epithets of praife or affection, fuch as " the gentle," or " the all-accomplifhed." Others have fhown the deeper appreciation of

---

* Murdin's Burghley Papers.

his worth, which is moſt feelingly expreſſed in the words of Camden:—" Of whom I çannot well ſay what and how much Britain augured for herſelf ; but ſnatched away by untimely death, he has been received into the ſacred aſſembly of heaven."

Among the elegies which were written on Sidney's death thoſe of Spenſer claim to be ſingled out for eſpecial notice. Very few poetical records of bereaved friendſhip ſurpaſs the grace of " Aſtrophel." Under Sidney's own adopted name and favourite diſguiſe of a ſhepherd, Spenſer deſcribes his friend's perſon and character, and relates allegorically the circumſtances of his death :—

> " A ſlender ſwain, excelling far each other
> In comely ſhape, like her that did him breed ;
>   He grew up faſt in goodneſs and in grace,
>   And doubly fair wox both in mind and face.

> " Which daily more and more he did augment,
> With gentle uſage and demeanour mild,
> That all men's hearts with ſecret raviſhment
> He ſtole away, and weetingly beguiled.
>   Nor ſpite itſelf, that all good things doth ſpill,
>   Found aught in him that ſhe could ſay was ill.

> " His ſports were fair, his joyaunce innocent,
> Sweet without ſour, and honey without gall ;
> And he himſelf ſeemed made for merriment,
> Merrily maſking both in bower and hall.
>   There was no pleaſure nor delightful play
>   When Aſtrophel ſo ever was away.

" In wreftling nimble, and in running fwift,
  In fhooting fteady, and in fwimming ftrong;
Well made to ftrike, to throw, to leap, to lift,
  And all the fports that fhepherds are among.
    In every one he vanquifhed every one;
    He vanquifhed all, and vanquifhed was of none."

With poetical licence, his wound is reprefented as caufed by the tufk of a boar in hunting, and his wife's perilous grief at his death is heightened to a fatal iffue :—

" His pallid face, impiétured with death,
  She bathed oft with tears, and dried oft;
And with fweet kiffes fucked the wafting breath
  Out of his lips, like lilies pale and foft:
    And oft fhe called to him, who anfwered nought,
    But only by his looks did tell his thought."

In defcribing her imaginary death the poet appropriates to her the name of Stella :—

" Forthwith her ghoft out of her corpfe did flit,
  And followed her mate like turtle chafte;
    To prove that death their hearts cannot divide,
    Which living were in love fo firmly tied.

" The gods, which all things fee, this fame beheld,
  And, pitying this pair of lovers true,
Transformed them, there lying on the field,
  Into a flower that is both red and blue:
    It firft grows red, and then to blue doth fade,
    Like Aftrophel, which thereunto was made.

" And in the midſt thereof a ſtar appears,
  As fairly formed as any ſtar in ſkies;
Reſembling Stella in her freſheſt years,
  Forth darting beams of beauty from her eyes;
    And all the day it ſtandeth full of dew,
      Which is the tears that from her eyes do flow."

But it was not only in this fantaſtic manner that Spenſer expreſſed his deep and ſincere regret. He often recurs to the theme of Sidney's virtues, in other poems. Thus, in his ſtately piece entitled " The Ruins of Time," while moralizing on the inſtability of human greatneſs, as illuſtrated by the deaths of the Earls of Leiceſter and Warwick, he takes occaſion to refer to Sidney in verſes of rare eloquence and ſweetneſs. Again, in his Sonnet to the Counteſs of Pembroke, he writes thus:—

" Remembrance of that moſt heroic ſpirit,
  The heaven's pride, the glory of our days,
Which now triumpheth, through immortal merit
  Of his brave virtues, crowned with laſting bays
Of heavenly bliſs and everlaſting praiſe;
  Who firſt my muſe did lift out of the floor,
To ſing his ſweet delights in lowly lays;
  Bids me, moſt noble lady, to adore
His goodly image, living evermore
  In the divine reſemblance of your face."

The collection of Spenſer's Works includes

feveral other poems, by various authors, appended to the elegy of " Aftrophel." One of thefe profeffes to be by the Countefs, " moft refembling, both in fhape and fpright, her brother dear," and is called " The Doleful Lay of Clorinda." It bears, however, apparent traces of Spenfer's thought and ftyle; as, for inftance, in the beautiful verfes which follow the queftion concerning Sidney's foul, " Ay me! can fo divine a thing be dead?"

" Ah, no! it is not dead, nor can it die,
 But lives for aye in blifsful Paradife:
Where, like a new-born babe, it foft doth lie,
 In bed of lilies wrapped in tender wife;
  And compaffed all about with rofes fweet,
  And dainty violets from head to feet.

" There thoufand birds, all of celeftial brood,
 To him do fweetly carol day and night,
And with ftrange notes, of him well underftood,
 Lull him afleep in angelic delight;
  Whilft in fweet dreams to him prefented be
  Immortal beauties, which no eye may fee."

Next in order come two pieces of which the reputed author is Lewis Bryfkett, a valued friend of Sidney, and his companion during his Italian tour. In the former of thefe, entitled " The Mourning Mufe of Theftylis," Sidney's laft

moments are defcribed with fome degree of rugged pathos. In the latter, called " A Paftoral
Eclogue," his death is lamented under the name
of Phillifides, by which Sidney refers to himfelf
in his Arcadia. Another elegy follows, by an
unknown author, and the feries is concluded by
two elaborate epitaphs, the former of which is by
far the beft, and is afcertained to be by Sir Walter
Raleigh,*

An obvious feature of all thefe elegies is a
ftrain of almoft idolatrous flattery, which has previoufly been noticed as a characteriftic of the age.
Yet, however faulty in point of truth or tafte
they may appear, the genuine refpect and love
which dictated them is unqueftionable. The
veneration with which Sidney was regarded was
doubtlefs increafed by the fplendid and tragical
circumftances of his death. Never did a mortal
ftroke appear more like the cruel work of the
" blind fury with the abhorred fhears," who " flits
the thinfpun life" of thofe who are about to find
the fair guerdon of fame. He lived long enough
to difplay a military genius to which, in England
at leaft, there was in that day no rival. For

---

* Butler's " Sidneiana." From this epitaph the mottoes to
Chapters I. and VII. are taken.

many years no fuccefs had been obtained, by an Englifh commander, of equal brilliancy and importance with the furprife of Axel; and it feemed that only opportunity was wanting to him to achieve ftill greater enterprifes. His youth added to the keennefs of regret with which his lofs was felt. Moft of thofe who leave a name to pofterity have fcarcely begun their public life, at the age when Sidney's career was brought to an end. His friends might well call his death untimely, in refpect of his promife for the national fervice; yet it was not altogether fo if we look to the growth and perfection of his character. We may aptly quote of him the kindly words which have recently been called forth by the deceafe of one of his race, heir alike of his name and virtues, the Chriftian gentleman, and the foldier's friend:—

> " O meafure not his life by length of days,
>   His thread is fully fpun, whom all unite to praife."

Sidney himfelf, being preffed overmuch by his fpiritual advifers to fay, whether he preferred to live or die, anfwered, " I do not grieve to die, and yet, to fpeak plainly, I rather wifh to live."* He was in the prime of phyfical vigour, when

---

* G. Whetftone, in Sir A. Bofwell's Collection of rare Poems.

the nature of man has full enjoyment of life, and abandons it moſt unwillingly.   He had, too, before his eyes, and under his hand, the taſk which had long loomed before him as the miſ-ſion to which he was called.   The grandeur of the conteſt with Spain had been understood by him with more than ordinary clearneſs.   He ſaw in it nothing leſs than a national ſtruggle for Liberty, and a religious ſtruggle for Truth.   With theſe deeper convictions a chivalrous love of glory intermingled.   The dim proſpect of ſuch exploits as followed ſhortly after his death had filled his mind with enthuſiaſm from childhood ; and he had only begun to taſte the felicity of him,—

> " who brought
> Among the taſks of real life, hath wrought
> Upon the plan that pleaſed his boyiſh thought."

Had his life been ſpared but a little while, he would have had an opportunity of joining with his friends in ſome of the moſt ſplendid achieve-ments recorded in Engliſh hiſtory.   He might have chaſed the Armada with Drake, and ſhared the fame of the capture of Cadiz with Raleigh and Eſſex.

Yet his early death removed him beyond the reach of worldly taint and corruption, and he escaped the ruin which befel several of the greatest of his contemporaries. Moreover, the very accident, which cut short his dreams of fame, gave to him an occasion of winning, far otherwise than he had conceived, a peerless rank in Christian knighthood. A just but happy destiny has associated for ever the name of Sidney with the anecdote of the wounded soldier. Neither history nor fiction contains any more beautiful example of the charity which the Gospel teaches. Yet the act was simply characteristic. Other men have lived who might have done the same, with more deliberate and continuous self-denial; but in Sidney's life this incident has a peculiar propriety, which leads one, in contemplating it, not so much to wonder, as to say, "How like him!" Among Christian worthies—and the foregoing narrative is a ground for applying this title to him—Sidney is distinguished by large and refined sympathy. At the Austrian Court, abridging his message of condolence out of regard for the Empress's sorrow; at home, refraining to visit Burleigh for fear that his presence should recall sad memories; conciliating the susceptible tempers of poets and men of letters, and retaining their universal love; in the Netherlands, pleading, at the peril of royal displeasure, on behalf of his poor foldiers; everywhere he fhows the fame exquifite fenfibility for others. Many delicate touches in his writings, which would be marred by quotation, no lefs than the importunity which fills his correfpondence, illuftrate this virtue, which, however fpontaneous it might feem in him, flowed from its true fource of love to God in Chrift. " He made the religion he profeffed the firm bafis of his life."

The completenefs of Sidney's charaéter is alfo remarkable. He bears to be regarded, like a well-executed ftatue, from all fides. Many good men are in comparifon like piétures, admirable when feen from one point of view, but having no other afpeét which claims attention. Their biographies are in confequence merely feleétions from their lives, of thofe things which friendfhip would wifh to hold in remembrance, with the omiffion of much that is effential: fo that fometimes the reader hardly knows them again, as they appear in the hiftory of their contemporaries. Such partial memoirs, where vital points of charaéter are fuppreffed, mifs the general end of biography, which is not to magnify individuals, but to compare humanity, as it is, with the image of God which is its perfeétion. But the effeét of a candid reprefentation is to make men feem worfe

than they really are, a difadvantage to which
Sidney is more expofed than moft, both from his
franknefs and from his verfatility. He lived with
his heart open to the world; and his fervid fpirit
led him into almoft every form of trial that can
befall a man. Soldier, ftatefman, diplomatift,
courtier, lover, poet, fcholar, philofopher, he is
liable to criticifm from every quarter where temp-
tation is ftrongeft and nature is moft frail. To
pafs through fuch an ordeal unfcathed would
argue fuperhuman virtue. It is much, under
fuch circumftances, to live unpolluted by the
darker fpots of fin, and to increafe with increafing
years in devotion and purity of foul. Some who,
with no more excufe, have fallen into guilt where
Sidney receded, have notwithftanding been en-
rolled among the faints. And if his chivalrous
renown fhould be turned to his difpraife, as feeming inconfiftent with the title of fanctity, the true
nature of the fpirit of chivalry muft be remembered. It was a fuperftition, blended of Chriftian and alien elements, which played in public
life a fimilar part to that which was filled by
monafticifm in retirement. Through ages of
darknefs and ferocity chivalry preferved the virtues of felf-denial, mercy, and gentlenefs. Like
monafticifm, it became obfolete in the advance

of civilization, and its abuſes increaſed as its good influence declined: but it was a living ſpirit in the days of Sidney, and in no one does chivalry look more fair. Upon the whole, he may be ſaid to come near to the ideal of an Engliſhman. His firſt principle was the love of truth, and what he ſeemed, he was to the very heart. He was a genuine patriot, a loyal lover of freedom, a brave and a wiſe gentleman; and while he was a type of what is nobleſt in his age and nation, his qualities were ſuch as have marked the greateſt and beſt men in all times.

PAMELA'S PRAYER.

Arcadia, Book III. See p. 96.

 ALL-SEEING Light, and eternal Life of all things, to whom nothing is either fo great that it may refift, or fo fmall that it is contemned: look upon my mifery with thine eye of mercy, and let thine infinite power vouchfafe to limit out fome proportion of deliverance unto me, as to thee fhall feem moft convenient. Let not injury, O Lord, triumph over me, and let my faults by thy hand be corrected, and make not mine enemy the minifter of thy juftice. But yet, O God, if, in thy wifdom, this be the apteft chaftifement for my inexcufable folly; if this low bondage be fitteft for my over-high defires; if the pride of my not enough humble heart be thus to be broken, O Lord, I yield unto thy will, and joyfully embrace what forrow thou wilt have me to fuffer. Only thus much let me crave of thee, —let my craving, O Lord, be accepted of thee, fince even that proceeds from thee,—let me crave (even by the nobleft title which in my great affliction I may give myfelf, that I am thy creature; and by thy goodnefs, which is thyfelf) that thou wilt fuffer fome beam of thy Majefty to fhine into my mind, that it may ftill depend confidently on thee. Let calamity be the exercife, but not the overthrow of my virtue: let their

power prevail, but prevail not to deſtruction.　Let my greatneſs be their prey; let my pain be the ſweetneſs of their
revenge; let them (if ſo ſeem good unto thee) vex me with
more and more puniſhment.　But, O Lord, let never their
wickedneſs have ſuch a hand, but that I may carry a pure mind
in a pure body!"

(From a Colle&ion of rare Poems privately printed by
Sir Alexander Bofwell.)

A Commemoration of the General Moan, and the Honourable and Solemn Funeral made for the Worthy Sir Philip Sidney, Kt., by B. W. Esq.

WHEN winter's bitter blaſt the trees began to bare,
Sweet Sidney ſlain, down fell our hope and pillar of welfare.
He was the riſing ſun, that made all England glad;
He was the light and life of thoſe that any virtues had;
He was the Muſes' joy, he was Bellona's ſhield,
Within the town he was a lamb, a lion in the field.
His life bewrayed a love that matched Curtius' zeal,
His death, no leſs contempt of death, to ſerve the common weal.
No gift nor grace there was, but in his virtues ſhined,
His worth, more worth than Flanders' wealth, now by his loſs we find.
For when his ſacred ſoul did forth his body fly,
Ten thouſand ſhrieks purſued the ſame into the ſtarry ſky:
The ſtouteſt ſoldiers, then, ſhowed feminine diſplay,
And with their tears did waſh his wound that brought him to decay.

R

Some kifled his breathlefs mouth, where wifdom flowed at will;
Some raifed his head that lately was the treafure-houfe of fkill.
Where truth and courage lived, his noble heart, fome felt;
Some laid their hands upon his breaft, where all the virtues
    dwelt.
Some eyed his clofen eyes, that watched the poor man's need,
And when they did unwrap his thigh, his wound did make
    them bleed.
" O honour dearly bought!" they cried, and moaned this
    chance,
So ftroke his hand, and faid, " Farewell, thou glory of the
    lance!"
Outcries foon fpread his death, the moan ran far and near,
What was he then, that mourned not the doleful news to hear?
The King of Scots bewrayed his grief in learned verfe,
And many more their paffions penned, with praife to deck his
    hearfe.
The Flufhingers made fuit his breathlefs corpfe to have,
And offered a fumptuous tomb the fame for to engrave;
But oh! his loving friends at their requeft did grieve,
It was too much he loft his life, his corfe they fhould not have.
And fo from Flufhing port, in fhip attired with black,
They did embark this perfect knight, that only breath did lack;
The wind and feas did mourn to fee this heavy fight,
And into Thames did carry this much lamented knight;
Unto the Minories his body was conveyed,
And then under a martial hearfe three months or more was
    laid;
But when the day was come he to his grave muft go,
An hoft of heavy men repaired to fee the folemn fhow:
The poor whom he, good knight, did often clothe and feed,
In frefh remembrance of their woe, went firft in mourning
    weed.

His friends and fervants fad was thought a heavy fight,
Who fixed their eyes upon the ground which now muſt houſe
    their knight.
To hear the drum and fife fend forth a doleful found,
To fee his colours, late advanced, lie trailing on the ground,
Each ornament of war thus out of order borne,
Did pierce ten thouſand hearts with grief, which were not
    named to mourn.
Some marked the great diſmay that charged his martial band,
And how ſome horſemen walked on foot, with battle-axe in
    hand.
Some told the mourning cloaks his gentlemen did wear,
What knights and captains were in gowns, and what the
    heralds bare ;
Some marked his ſtately horſes how they hung down their head,
As if they mourned for their knight that followed after dead.
But when his noble corſe in ſolemn wiſe paſſed by,
" Farewell the worthieſt knight that lived !" the multitude did
    cry ;
" Farewell, that honoured art by laurel and the lance !
" Farewell the friend beloved of all, that hadſt no foe but
    chance ! "
His ſolemn funeral, befeeming his eſtate,
Was by the heralds marſhalled, the more to mourn his fate.
Three Earls and other Lords, the Holland States in black,
With all their train, then followed ; and that no love might
    lack,
The Mayor and Aldermen in purple robes then mourned,
And laſt a band of citizens, with weapons awkward turned,
In ſolemn wiſe did bring this knight unto the ground ;
Who being then beſtowed at reſt, their laſt adieu to found,
Two vollies of brave ſhot they thundered to the ſkies ;
And thus his funeral did end with many weeping eyes ;

Upon whofe monument in letters writ with gold
This epitaph deferves to be, for all men to behold.

Of the moft worthy and hardy knight, Sir Philip Sidney,
THE EPITAPH.

Here underneath lies PHILIP SIDNEY, Knight,
True to his Prince, learned, ftaid, and wife,
Who loft his life in honourable fight,
Who vanquifhed death, in that he did defpife
To live in pomp by others brought to pafs,
Which oft he termed a diamond fet in brafs.

THE END.

CHISWICK PRESS.—PRINTED BY WHITTINGHAM AND WILKINS,
TOOKS COURT, CHANCERY LANE.